C000076036

HOW
HARSH MARIWALA
'GROOMED'
MARICO

HOW HARSH MARIWALA 'GROOMED' MARICO

R. Gopalakrishnan
M. Suresh Rao

RUPA

Published by
Rupa Publications India Pvt. Ltd 2021
7/16, Ansari Road, Daryaganj
New Delhi 110002

Sales Centres:
Allahabad Bengaluru Chennai
Hyderabad Jaipur Kathmandu
Kolkata Mumbai

ISBN: 978-93-90260-23-2

First impression 2021

10 9 8 7 6 5 4 3 2 1

The moral right of the authors have been asserted.

Printed at Parksons Graphics Pvt. Ltd., Mumbai.

Contents

Preface

The activity of making and marketing everyday household products like soap, toothpaste or oil is commonly regarded as frivolous and light in terms of technology, unlike corporate ventures engaged in the automotive, infrastructure or engineering sectors. One cannot oppose this view that perceives the breathtaking sweep of a bridge over the gushing power of a river, or the revving power of a truck, or even the sophistication of a piece of software, with far more adulation and gasps than a face cream or a bottle of hair oil.

It would, however, be wrong to presume that fast-moving consumer companies do not deploy complex technologies to successfully manage business operations as a comprehensive model, right from research and production to marketing, distribution and customer service. In fact, such companies must master a whole business model comprising the supply chain, manufacturing, distribution and, above all, the art of tempting both the fickle and the reluctant-to-change consumer. Complexity is, thus, not only contained in the technology visibly driving the product, but lies in the invisible end-to-end business model, comprising deep immersion into the arenas of physical sciences, psychology, sociology, communications and logistics. These aspects are not easily recognized by the mindset of a developing nation. No wonder then, that since early times, fast-moving consumer goods (FMCG) have been perceived as low value, dispensable and lacking in technology.

Following India's Independence, for instance, when the nation found itself short of precious foreign exchange, products like face powder and eye-liner were the first few items of import to be banned. Hapless and distressed Indian women approached Indira Gandhi, who was a resident in the house of Prime Minister Jawaharlal Nehru. Their complaint was that Indian women led a tough life, completely free of indulgences, and therefore, the harmless and minor indulgence of a dash of face powder should not be denied to them. The young leader initiated a call to an Indian business house. Tata Industries Resident Director in Delhi, Kish Naoroji,[1] was quizzed about why such products could not be manufactured and made available domestically. This question led to a spate of actions by the Tata Oil Mills Company (TOMCO) and the birth of Lakme Limited in Bombay (present-day Mumbai) in the 1960s.

Another example that shows it is not easy to run an FMCG company involves two talented engineers, who graduated with advanced degrees in chemical technology from an American University in 1949. Shortly thereafter, they returned to India. While one engineer joined the newly set up Atomic Energy Establishment, the other joined Hindustan Vanaspati Manufacturing company (now

---

[1]Tata Luminaries. Accessed from http://www.tatacentralarchives.com/tata-legacy/luminaries.html

Hindustan Unilever—HUL). The Atomic Energy engineer got involved in heavy water and nuclear reactors, while the HUL engineer learnt about hydrogenation and saponification. They kept in touch, although the atomic engineer would tease the HUL engineer that he was only dealing with basic processes and products despite an advanced degree from the US.

Decades later, the atomic engineer, Homi Sethna, rose to the position of Chairman of Atomic Energy, and the HUL engineer, Vasant Rajadhyaksha, became HUL chairman. In due course, both retired from their chairmanships. However, in a piquant reversal of roles, Sethna became a Tata director, and among his responsibilities was the chairmanship of TOMCO, while Rajadhyaksha joined the Planning Commission of India. Sethna, in his new position, could not figure out why TOMCO ran losses year after year while Hindustan Lever (HLL) continued to flourish. Sethna then sought the counsel of his old friend, Rajadhyaksha, on how to turn TOMCO around. Rajadhyaksha had a quiet laugh because his friend Homi had finally realized that it was not as easy to run an FMCG as he had presumed. However, in a cruel irony of fate, the Tatas sold TOMCO to HLL in 1993.

Yet another instance shows up the much-maligned reputation of FMCG companies. In the 1970s, the Government of India passed a legislation called the Foreign Exchange Regulation Act (FERA), which compelled 'low technology' companies to dilute foreign shareholding to 40 per cent unless it could fulfil certain conditions. This legislation marked out consumer goods giant, HLL, which after long and complex negotiations with the government, reached an agreement under which its foreign partner Unilever could hold 51 per cent as it fulfilled the specified conditions.[2] However, as a former HLL senior board member recalls, 'Government officers often joked about HLL's case. On one occasion, the Reserve Bank governor prodded the HLL chairman, in jest, "So is your company still making soap?" The HLL chairman replied, "Most certainly, Governor, so that you can bathe every day".'

These anecdotes illustrate how the popular perception of FMCG companies being lightweight in terms of technology is deeply entrenched in the Indian psyche. Few realize that although every domain has its own specialty, it is incredibly complex to launch and establish a distinctive brand, build up its value and market share and hold the pole position over a long time—just as difficult as it is to build complex bridges and nuclear reactors. It is also not well known that successful FMCG companies require relatively less capital for investment in manufacturing plants, machinery, equipment and other fixed assets. Due to the high turnover to investment ratio, these companies are steady market performers and provide a relatively safe haven for investors, besides getting a far better stock market valuation as compared to other categories of companies. The mouthwatering earnings multiple belongs more in the realm of FMCG companies than road-builders and equipment manufacturers. Markets don't lie; certainly they have not for decades and across countries.

One such FMCG company is Marico, which evolved from Bombay Oil Industries Limited (BOIL), a family-owned start-

---

[2]Shashank Shah, *Win-Win Corporations: The Indian Way of Shaping Successful Strategies*, Portfolio, 2016.

up at the time of India's Independence. The story of Marico, which follows in this book, is an outstanding example of the trials and tribulations of a home-grown FMCG venture, which earned a prized market value of US $6.7 billion (February 2019) in the four decades of its existence, despite international competition in the Indian market. Practising and institutionalizing aspired and virtuous management actions do not come easily to any organization, especially one born from the womb of a traditional bulk commodity, family-owned business, 150 years ago.

As the scion of this business family, Harsh Mariwala[3] accomplished the differentiation between a commodity and a brand by being agile, spotting blue ocean spaces, developing consumer insight, manufacturing and distribution development through trial and error, and inducting professionals and top-class governance, besides instilling humility and a learning attitude—certainly not easy accomplishments by any standards.

As authors, we enjoyed interviewing Mariwala and numerous Marico stakeholders. We hope that the reader will enjoy the read as much as learn from this book, recounting the trials and tribulations of the Mariwala family odyssey. What began as a spice-trading venture, morphed into the export of spice extracts and extended to manufacturing commodities, before evolving as a remarkable tryst with branding.

---

[3]Referred in this book as either Harsh or Mariwala

Chapter 1

The Mariwala Family Odyssey

The Mariwala family traces its business origin as traders in spices since the late nineteenth century. And where else can you source spices other than from Kerala?

Since ancient times, Kerala has been a hotbed of several species of exotic spices, much sought after by the world for garnishing their food. Historically, global seafarers and traders, including the Babylonians, Egyptians, Arabs, Chinese and Europeans, connected with Kerala and established the two-millennia-old Spice Route,[1] making this region a true melting pot of culture and civilization. Even Gujarati businessmen fleeing from Mohammed of Ghazni's invasion of Gujarat in the eleventh century reached Kerala by sea. Soon, they started trading. They brought textiles and other items from Gujarat and exported spices and copra (dried coconut kernels) from Kerala. Eventually, they settled in the coastal cities of Kerala. Some even set up value-adding processing units near the spice-growing areas.[2] It is, in fact, believed

---

[1]International Spice Route Project report on Kerala
[2]delhipost.com, 27 February 2008

1

that it was a Gujarati named Ram Chandra Malan, a pepper trader, who guided Vasco da Gama, the Portuguese explorer, when he arrived in Kozhikode in 1498 and established a sea route to Kerala by setting up a Portuguese presence to colonize Kerala. Apparently, trade relations between the rulers of Calicut and Cochin, and the Portuguese, were facilitated by members of the Gujarati community.[3] Present-day settlements of the Gujarati community in Kerala in places like Fort Kochi and Mattancherry date back to 1813, around the end of East India Company's monopoly in global trade. These settlements developed into flourishing commercial hubs for export of spices and other commodities. Although today the business is dwindling, Kerala's domination over this commodity continues, with three-fourths of spice exports from India being generated from the state. Historically, the spice trade drew people from near and far.

SPICE TRADERS

The recorded origin of the Mariwala family can be traced to two brothers from Kutch district in present-day Gujarat. In 1872, still in their teens and with pockets full of high hopes, Kanji and Vasanji set out to make their fortune in distant Bombay, only to eke a living by hand, stitching gunny bags. Undismayed, yet seeking better opportunities, they soon job-hopped to first hoist cotton bales onto weighing machines and then morphed into cotton brokers. In 1887, the enterprising brothers had 'arrived' in Kerala, setting up a spice-trading

---

[3]Secretary of Gujarati Mahajan Cochin (1883) in delhipost.com

firm with Khetsi, a fellow Gujarati.

The business prospered and in 1896, Vasanji became the proud father of Vallabhdas, the next generation and Harsh's grandfather. However, Vasanji passed away soon thereafter, leaving young Vallabhdas in the care of his brother, Kanjibhai. Vallabhdas soon joined his uncle in the business. Around 1916, two important events happened. Vallabhdas married and the uncle-nephew duo dissolved the parent firm and started business afresh as commission agents, dealing in commodities such as ginger, turmeric, copra and spice, which were transported and sold in the big city of Bombay for the local traders. The agency built for itself a reputation for integrity and commitment among the trading community in Kerala.

Meanwhile, observing that Kutchi families did not have surnames—the father's name being tagged to the individual's name—the British Government in 1911 decided to allocate surnames to everyone. All traders were bestowed the surname of 'Merchant' and in the process, Vallabhdas Vasanji emerged as V.V. Merchant. Expectedly, the profusion of 'Merchants' created mayhem, which led to surname changes. Thus, V.V. Merchant transformed to Vallabhdas Vasanji Mariwala, alias 'Pepperman' or one who deals in pepper. In Gujarati, 'mari' means pepper, a prominent item in their trading portfolio, hence the name. This surname survived through the succeeding generations. Vallabhdas went on to have 10 children—four sons and six daughters. The sons went on to manage and expand the business. After all, business ran in their bloodline.

MOVING INTO MANUFACTURING

Vallabhdas's eldest son, Charandas, joined the business while still studying in college. He was a quick learner who set his sights beyond the world of trading. Charandas could anticipate the gains in moving up the value chain through manufacturing. He celebrated India's Independence by starting BOIL. In true Mariwala tradition, the company's shares were closely held within the Mariwala family.

BOIL established four manufacturing units between 1947 and 1971, with three in Mumbai and one in Kerala. The company operated the existing spice-processing facility as a spice extraction plant in the palm-fringed backwaters of Alleppey near Cochin. Export of spice extracts generated substantial revenues and profits that transformed the company. BOIL eventually commanded 20 per cent of the global market for spice extracts. The company also acquired a vanaspati (thick edible oil) factory and a solvent extraction plant to extract residual oil from oil cakes for export. It commenced operations for extraction of coconut oil from quality copra, and shortly thereafter, it launched a refinery to refine edible oil from safflower. Looking back, Harsh Mariwala salutes his father's and uncle's foresight in anticipating the market demand for safflower oil owing to its health benefits.

BOIL extended its operations by venturing into manufacturing finished consumer products: Parachute Coconut Oil (named after the World War II parachutes—a novelty for the subcontinent that denoted safety and reliability) and Saffola Edible Oil, made from safflower. These oils were sold to distributors in large, 15-litre tins. The price and margins were reasonable, as was the offtake by trade.

Additionally, BOIL set up a chemical plant to produce oleochemicals, a common material used in the formulation and production of household, industrial and institutional 'clean and care' items such as surface cleaners, fabric cleaners and softeners, dishwashing and automotive care products, besides degreasers and other intermediates.

In time, the company acquired a reputation for the quality of its products. Parachute established itself as a superior-quality coconut oil. Its reputation was based on the aroma, purity and clarity of the product and the processes instituted for ensuring consistency in quality. Charandas managed the greatly diversified businesses under BOIL with his three brothers.

BOIL was a typical family business and the extended Mariwala family lived together, sharing a common kitchen in a sprawling, five-storeyed bungalow facing the Arabian sea at Haji Ali in Worli, Mumbai. Whether in business or on the home front, everything was shared. It was understood that the children growing up in the Mariwala family fold shall join the family business after completing their education—the earlier the better.

ENTER HARSH MARIWALA

Harsh, Charandas's eldest son, spent his growing up years in the milieu of a joint family of 25-plus members. While there was a lot of bonding and family time together, Harsh recollects that as the eldest from the third generation he had many duties and obligations like seeing off and welcoming returning family members from overseas. In true Hindu joint family tradition, he learnt to become flexible and more tolerant while being able to adjust to the needs of others. Little known to him, this trait of patience and flexibility was to stand him in good stead during the challenging years leading up to the weaning away of Marico from its parent company, BOIL.

Unlike his outgoing father, young Harsh was, in his description of himself, an introvert, average in studies, unsure of himself and scared to speak in public forums. Yet, notwithstanding his diffidence, he always thought, 'I have to be in business', rather than 'I would work for someone else'. Harsh completed his graduation in Commerce from Sydenham College.

He could not clear the MBA exams for admission to a reputed business school, and Charandas turned down his request to pursue an MBA overseas. Perhaps apprehensive that his son might be enticed to marry a foreigner and forsake his home and country, Charandas was keen to initiate him into the family business. However, feeling that Harsh could have a break before committing to business, he was allowed to set off with a companion on a 45-day jaunt of America and Europe prior to being inducted into the business in 1971.

At the end of the trip, while his companion Pradeep Harlalka's bag was brimming with goodies, perfumes, clothes and chocolates, Harsh's virgin mind was brimming with the possibilities for branded consumer products back home—so impressed was he observing the display stacks of supermarkets in America. Returning to Bombay, he shed all thoughts of the noisy, overcrowded lanes of Masjid Bunder where the office of BOIL was located and looked forward to a life devoted to branded business.

Before him, Kanji, Vassanji and Vallabhdas—Harsh's forefathers—had earned their spurs as spice traders. Harsh's father Charandas set up BOIL to become a manufacturer of consumer goods, among other products—the coconut oil and the safflower-based oil, named Parachute and Saffola, respectively. What fired his imagination was the opportunity for branding consumer products at a time when the general impression in India was that edible oils were 'home-grown' products made by local companies, and brands were the preserve of multinational FMCG companies.

Was the young Harsh, the first member of the fourth generation of Mariwalas, conscious of his destiny the day he entered BOIL as an intern? 'I didn't have any clue when I joined the business what I'm going to do. When they say, "You have to have a dream and a vision," I think it develops over a period of time,'[4] Mariwala recalled. Quite clearly for him, while it was acceptable to daydream at leisure, it had no place at work. Here, the priority was to learn the ropes of doing business. So, starting his internship, Harsh, the protagonist of this book, immersed himself in the nitty-gritty of BOIL's various businesses from day one, as we shall see in the next chapter.

---

[4]The Neeraj Shah Show, Season 1, Episode 2, Mariwala's recollection during his interview with Neeraj Shah, published 7 September 2016

Chapter 2

Grassroots Learning

Harsh was not a first-generation entrepreneur starting from scratch; he was very much a scion of a business family—an Indian manufacturer of consumer oils—now in its fourth generation. He spent almost two decades at BOIL, raising the consumer oils division from relative obscurity to the largest and most profitable business for BOIL, before venturing out to create Marico as his contribution to the group business. All the while learning on the job, he made a successful foray into branding commodity products in a pioneering journey, especially at a time when branding was still in its infancy in India.

What is the significance of branding for the FMCG sector? A rhetorical question today, but not so 75 years ago, given that branding was barely known in India then. For the record, branding made its debut in India with Sunlight (soap) around 1890. However, it was only in the second half of the twentieth century that Indian brands began impacting consumers. Shackled as the country was with the deadweight of imperialism, all attempts at creating an FMCG industry were choked.

Was branding an outcome of the market revolution in the 1820s that witnessed the rise of mass production and shipment of trade goods? Was it the need to stand out in the crowd by creating an identity that evolved into a trademark, recognition of which led to the development of a brand?

EVOLUTION OF BRANDING

The birth of branding can be traced to product identification that developed when customers felt the need for it. For example, customers in New York City learned to choose bread loaves from the street vendor, based on the full weight symbols marked on the loaf by the bakers. Such basic differentiation helped to identify the maker of the product, seek quality assurance and hold the maker responsible—all of which resonate even today as the benchmark for a brand. The genesis of the evolution of product identity to a brand may be connected with Procter & Gamble, the world's oldest FMCG company.

Marketing historians trace the branding of FMCG to two US immigrants, William Procter from England and James Gamble from Ireland, who met to pursue their destiny in Cincinnati, USA. Their spouses were sisters and prodded by their common father-in-law, they founded their venture Procter & Gamble (P&G) in October 1837. The company made and marketed candles and soap. The company's trademark of moon and stars developed by chance when illiterate workers, to distinguish between boxes of candles and soaps, marked candle boxes with a crude 'X', which was changed to a circle around a star and then modified to a man in the moon.

Candles were a commodity item, but customers gradually

started to identify P&G marked boxes as the preferred product, leading to the rejection of an entire shipment of candles without the 'man in the moon' mark as an imitation. This incident moved P&G to register a modified version of the wharf hand's design as a trademark that showed a man in the moon overlooking 13 stars, to commemorate the original 13 American colonies. This trademark became the logo of P&G, which helped to create its Ivory white soap—conceptualized around the theme of purity. Advertising differentiated this soap from others and once identified by customers, it quickly became a strong customer brand.[5] This could well have been the origin of branding, which would take much longer to reach India, still in the midst of its struggle with imperialism.

CONSUMER INDIA AWAKENS

In the early decades post-Independence, breathing the air of freedom, India focused on its recovery from devastation and poverty in the wake of the British Raj and the Partition of India. In this era, FMCG[6] in India were majorly commodities, purchased from the local kirana or grocery store for regular consumption. Middle-class India managed with mass consumption products that were ubiquitous, affordable and often trademarked.

On the brighter side of consumerism, there was exposure to rural skills through cottage industry emporiums to market

---

[5]Julia Pennington and Dwayne Ball, 'Customer branding of commodity products: The customer developed brand' , *Journal of Brand Management*, June 2009

[6]The terms 'FMCG' and 'consumer products' are used interchangeably.

branded handloom and handicrafts, made by artisans and weavers displaced during the Partition as well as a nationwide marketing of branded petrol by Indian Oil Corporation, Bharat Petroleum and Hindustan Petroleum. Air travel was made popular by Indian Airlines and Air India. In this era, trend setters for consumerism like Modern Bread, HMT Janata watch and Sahakari Bhandar (a chain of general stores in Mumbai) were providing genuine value-for-money products for the middle class. Ironically, all were state government undertakings!

Unfortunately, the trend towards middle-class consumerism was halted in its tracks by creeping socialism masquerading as a 'mixed economy' and the Planning Commission becoming the arbiter of consumer choice in place of the marketplace. The all-pervasive sovereignty of the 'license-permit-quota Raj' translated into scarcity for the consumer, who was unable to afford goods sold in the black market.[7] Availability of consumer products was stretched due to the cumulative effects of a number of drawbacks: underdeveloped infrastructure and logistics and paucity of reliable trade partners, besides the near absence of banking support to trade.

Making do with brands was not for everyone. Commodities accounted for the needs of 98 per cent of the population while brands served a measly 2 per cent. The prevailing impression was that commodities were for the common people, or aam junta, and brands for the well-to-do.

Expansion of branded consumer products, thus, faced

---

[7]C. Rajagopalachari (Rajaji) in his writings for the journal *Swatantra*

severe challenges in the socialist era. Looking back, one wonders at the bravado of marketing professors of that era to expound on marketing mantras like segmenting, targeting, positioning and branding, or the 4Ps of marketing—Product, Price, Place and Promotion—within the classroom, stoically unconcerned with the restrictive environment outside! The absence of experienced copywriters with ad agencies also led to challenges in creating meaningful and engaging value propositions to hook consumers, all of which resulted in much less money being allocated for marketing by companies— crucial for brand building.

Fortunately, the winds of change favouring liberalism were blowing across the globe. India was no exception to its impact, registering hope that the 'dark age' would soon fade away.

BRAND CONSCIOUSNESS

As India stepped into the 1990s, the government initiated policies that freed the economy from controls, ushering capacity increase and competition to serve the pent-up desires of the people. Indians began to happily to take on the 'big, bad world' of branded FMCG.

Branded consumer products were packaged. They captured customer attention on the store shelf, flaunted a brand name and logo, and were promoted extensively through catchy jingles across media. In fact, jingles were an intrinsic part of brand promotion in India, more so than most countries, possibly linked to the association of songs with memorable films that fared well at the turnstiles. Thus, for families living in metro cities, brand presence was mostly represented by the musical lilt of Sunlight washing soap, the first Unilever brand in India, which heralded the arrival of branded consumer products in the country. Some memorable jingles went on to attain signature status for products—for example, Lifebuoy body soap (*Lifebuoy hai jahan, tandurusti hae wahan*); Amul butter (*Taste of India*, urging Indians to adopt bread and butter for breakfast); Bajaj scooter (*Hamara Bajaj*); and Saridon, the headache pill (*Na rahey peeda, na rahey dard, sirf ek Saridon*).

Gradually, corporate India understood that with deft marketing, any accepted consumer product with a name and perceived as a commodity, could be transformed into a 'brand', a classic illustration of those times being the birth of Cinthol soap from Godrej Soaps (Godrej Consumer Products). Cinthol soap, a dull, yet rock solid and long-lasting product, demonstrated its transition from a commodity—the lower rungs of the brand pyramid—to the top of the heap as a brand infused with functional and emotional benefits. Besides deft marketing, the product itself went through a turnaround and vaulted from a stolid, 'colourless' product to a soap with better lather and 'best looks'. Its new packaging went through a dramatic change. Cinthol's image transformed from boring to glamourous when the dashing cricketer Imran Khan was roped in as brand ambassador to the accompaniment of high media visibility.

This was around the time when young Harsh was out on the field, soaking in ideas on the transformational possibilities of marketing Parachute as an FMCG brand. He absorbed marketing insights from a variety of sources, including his

American exposure to retail, during his brief overseas sojourn. He was deeply impacted by the supermarkets in America that overflowed with attractively packaged and eye-catching consumer brands, an impression that would significantly shape his belief in consumer marketing. Other sources were reading, attending seminars and seeking inputs from mentors and marketing consultants. Harsh picked up the basics of consumer product marketing in this manner and learned in particular from Professor Labdhi Bhandari, Marketing faculty at the Indian Institute of Management (IIM) Ahmedabad and recognized as a leading marketing mind in the country, with the know-how of converting a commodity to a brand. His mind brimmed with the possibilities for branded consumer products from BOIL.

HANDS-ON BUSINESS

For young Harsh, 21 years old and fresh from college, life as an intern at BOIL was a voyage of discovering business unaided by any training process. From day 1 of his induction into the family business, one bright morning in 1971, Harsh immersed himself in the nitty-gritty of understanding BOIL's various businesses. He interned with each of the manufacturing divisions—the processing of spices, the refining of coconut oil and safflower oil and the making of oleochemicals, managed by Charandas and his brothers—to understand business operations. His enquiring mind sought answers that stood him in good stead in later years. The oleochemicals and spice extracts manufactured by BOIL were intermediate products marketed directly as business-to-business (B2B). Coconut and safflower oils were categorized as finished products, ready for consumption by the customer and marketed through business-to-consumer channels.

Located in the noisy overcrowded lanes of Masjid Bunder in Mumbai, BOIL functioned as a traditional family business. It sold Parachute and Saffola oil in bulk to its distributors as a B2B transaction, at a price that was acceptable to distributors while covering costs and leaving a modest margin for BOIL.

With unquestioned access at BOIL as a member of the family, Harsh soon realized how 'family-iarly' the business functioned! He saw that access to the family was important to man senior-level positions and 'work' happily ever after in the company—one general manager for instance, was his uncle's teacher. Consequently, most employees learned on the job, with the exception of the head of manufacturing who was perhaps the only employee technically qualified for the responsibility. Other aspects of this home-grown business were that no data was maintained on product costing, none of the jobs had key result areas and investments were not the result of financial projections. It was accepted that in some years, the business would generate profit, while losses in other years—the cause being attributed to raw material price fluctuations, an external factor.

GOING THE EXTRA MILE

Harsh devoted his time and effort towards understanding the sales and distribution function for the two consumer products. He made extensive field tours to various districts in Maharashtra and Gujarat, connecting with distributors, retailers and users of Parachute oil. He observed that Parachute was being marketed by default as a commodity product to distributors, in large tin containers. The trade practice was to supply the oil in bulk to distributors in major cities who would sell it to retailers, who would re-pack the oil for eventual purchase by the consumer in a 'loose' format.

Harsh also sought to understand customers' perception about the purchase and usage of Parachute coconut oil. How much was the choice casual or intentional? In the course of his field visits to smaller towns, he had the opportunity to 'market research' the perception of Parachute held by channel members, that is the distributors, retailers and their staff, besides customers. He found that although externally they may not have been able to distinguish Parachute from others, as all coconut oils at the time came packaged in wholesale tins sold loose by retailers, customers favoured Parachute and the modestly higher price was not a deterrent for regular purchasers. He discovered their 'clear' preference for Parachute over other options in the market in terms of purity, clarity and aroma. Harsh correlated this preference with the product attributes of using the finest grade of copra supported by quality processes for oil refining. This commitment to quality was an article of faith for the owners. Not surprising, then, for Parachute to enjoy leading market share.

Harsh also observed that despite the superior features of Parachute coconut oil that had found favour with customers, there was no national awareness for any coconut oil brand, except in east India for a brand named Shalimar. Harsh travelled east to check out Parachute's competitor in Bengal. Touring Bengal, he noticed that Shalimar was being sold to customers in family pack tins. Shalimar Oils, a Kolkata-based company and a recent player in the same category of coconut oil as Parachute, was successfully marketing the oil as a branded customer product to retail, at a time when there was no other branded coconut oil in the country. The brand had a major share of the market in the eastern region.

Observing trade and the consumer acceptance of premium pricing for branded products, whether foreign or Indian, Harsh realized that BOIL's consumer products—Parachute and Saffola—were undersold. They had high acceptance in the market but were not perceived as brands either by distributors or customers. Or, for that matter, even by the management of BOIL.

Management indifference to marketing and in keeping track of trade behaviour could impact Parachute's reputation for quality. During his field visit to Vidarbha in Maharashtra, for instance, Harsh had observed that while the company sold Parachute oil in 15 litre tins to distributors, customers were buying the oil in 'loose' format, thereby raising the disconcerting possibility of compromising quality through adulteration. Some distributors also resold Parachute in smaller tins through their own initiative. Harsh realized that effectively, the benefit of the premium image of the brand was reaped more by the trade and not so much by BOIL, given the prevalent marketing outlook of the company management. For the Mariwala family, quality and product features were what mattered to generate sales. Also, not being marketers working in the field or in everyday touch with either the retailers who sold directly to customers or with the customers themselves, the family was unable to feel the pull of the product in the market.

This hands-on experience of BOIL's business in the field convinced Mariwala that Parachute was differentiated from other coconut oils, which was unfortunately perceived by the family management as a quality commodity with no brand aura around it. Harsh had a vision of transforming Parachute to a coveted brand. Insights gained on the field and reaching out to customers at the retail level proved invaluable for branding Parachute.

This was the first time a member of the Mariwala clan had set foot on the field and held extensive interactions with sales staff, distributors and retailers, besides discussions with customers. Regular visits to the market, observation of trade behaviour and feedback from field staff set him apart from his family. Harsh felt he was now equipped with the 'know-how' of channel management for FMCG. He generously credits the trade channel in the inhospitable climes of Vidarbha, which he visited in the heat of summer and the chill of winter, for instilling in him the basics of managing markets. The experience brought forth observations and ideas that were, for the conventional Mariwala family, quite revolutionary.

THE KNOWLEDGE SEEKER

Since his early days in BOIL, in addition to field visits, Harsh spared no efforts in picking up business know-how and insights, particularly marketing and business strategy, from diverse sources. He sought professional help to make up for his own lack of formal business knowledge and its absence within the family.

Through the 1970s, Harsh consulted experts in four key functions of the FMCG business: marketing and branding, advertising, distribution and the HR function. He consulted Professor Bhandari for consumer marketing and branding. Although Professor Bhandari was a consultant for corporates, Harsh sought him out to gain insights on branding consumer products, keenly aware that the consumer products division of BOIL was yet a small-scale enterprise (SME) with its office located in the midst of Mumbai's commodity markets. His earnestness induced the academic to accept the assignment to 'teach' the SME businessman, harbouring big-time aspirations, the benefits of designing a branding strategy for BOIL's consumer products. To match Professor Bhandari's exacting work schedule, Harsh willingly adjusted his own availability. He would meet the Professor at Mumbai airport, catch the flight with him to Ahmedabad, where they would work through the night and next morning, Harsh would fly back to Mumbai!

For insights into FMCG advertising, Harsh consulted one of Mumbai's premier ad agencies, Clarion Advertising. For the HR function, he sought out his friend Homi Mulla, HR Head at Monsanto, and for distribution, he recruited a veteran from Hindustan Unilever. Harsh used this network as a sounding board for developing or discarding his ideas on building the consumer product division of BOIL.

Harsh's exposure to the external world through reading, participating in seminars and interaction with experts influenced his mind to modern concepts in business. His experiences on the field convinced him that, given a quality product with differentiated benefits vis-à-vis competition, branding combined with extensive distribution was key to the sustained success for consumer product companies. He realized that manufacturing was not a holy cow, and under appropriate circumstances one could consider outsourcing too, as manufacturing was not the only stage where branded consumer product companies added value. Harsh's keen determination in pursuing his objective of differentiating the family-run business from his competitors contrasted with the quiet acceptance of the status quo by his contented family members.

ACHIEVING FAMILY BUY-IN

When it came to choosing his area of work in BOIL after his internship and field experiences, Harsh opted for the consumer products division, which comprised Parachute coconut oil and Saffola edible oil. Brimming with ideas, Harsh wanted to execute changes bottom-up across functions. Leveraging the learnings from his interactions with Professor Bhandari, Harsh actioned a plan for higher sales and profitability of Parachute and Saffola. This was an opportunity for him to earn his spurs in branding BOIL's consumer products. His on-field experiences combined with his exposure to American supermarkets triggered in his mind, an aspiration of what could be achieved through branding and cultivation of retail. He wanted to develop consumer product marketing for BOIL and looked forward to a life devoted to branded businesses.

The Mariwala family, however, had different views. Selling to distributors was the accepted Mariwala way of doing business. At heart, the family preferred the manufacturing model to shifting gears to a marketing-biased model. Besides the lack of appreciation for marketing as a value-adding function, the family seemed satisfied with the success achieved by transforming the age-old business of trading to higher value-adding manufacturing. The family consensus was against the shift in functional emphasis from manufacturing to marketing as that would require extensive efforts and expenditure in advertising, sales staffing and trade-related costs, adversely impacting BOIL's steady progress through focus on operations.

Harsh, however, was determined, and with patience and persistence, set out to transform the views of the family through persuasive discussions. He shared with the family his observations during his travels across east India, on how Shalimar, a regional brand, was able to extract higher margins and greater market share through branding. Another issue for discussion among the family was the breakthrough efforts of the founders of Asian Paints in elevating the company to market leadership by their pioneering strategy of branding and extensive retail reach for consumer paints. Harsh would emphasize that the 'success stories' of Shalimar Oil and Asian Paints could be replicated by BOIL for Parachute and Saffola, as both these products shared the common criteria of quality, scale and consumer acceptance.

To persuade his family, Harsh's approach for bringing about change was through step-by-step incremental innovation. For product development, he would coordinate with his research and development (R&D) team, conceptualize product features, test and pivot the prototype, release it in the local market for market acceptance and then launch the product, state by state. Initiatives had to be manageable to restrict any loss within affordable limits. This approach won the 'buy-in' from the family.

His disposition toward consumer marketing differentiated him from his family members who were happily immune to the notion of branding. Remember, BOIL was achieving steady growth selling oil in bulk to distributors as a B2B transaction, besides its other businesses?

Yet, taking along his family with every move, Harsh nurtured the seed of Marico to a sapling in the soil of BOIL, before moving it out, with the blessings of his family. He pursued his passion of creating and nurturing brands, which would impact lives and enrich the story of consumer branding in India, with single-minded determination and in the process, architectured Marico as a business institution. The saga of branding and Harsh's magnificent obsession with brands unfolds in the subsequent chapter.

Chapter 3

Mariwala's Magnificent Obsession

Harsh's first three years in BOIL were slow and steady. He learnt the ropes of the businesses that BOIL owned. In the process, he perceived the opportunity for transforming Parachute and Saffola as national, household brands. Eager to put his game plan into action, Harsh crafted a makeover strategy for consumer products from the ground up and worked on strengthening the products' packaging and marketing. The company grew as he expanded distribution and nurtured the strategy to fruition and Parachute and Saffola became leading brands.

BRANDING PARACHUTE

The key elements of Harsh's strategy were to offer Parachute in a smaller family pack size, extend availability pan-India through an expanded network of dealers and advertise widely in key areas to capture consumer acceptance for the brand.

Going Small for Big Sales: Three years into being baptized in the business, Harsh persuaded the family to implement the breakthrough idea of selling Parachute coconut oil in family-size branded tins to retail stores, thus bringing the brand directly to the consumer through retailers. He focused his initial efforts in increasing sales in BOIL's backyard of Maharashtra and Gujarat by appointing distributors and retailers where Parachute was under-represented.

The company changed its marketing strategy from a B2B marketing model to B2C marketing as befits a branded consumer product. In retrospect, changing focus from selling in bulk to distributors to directly marketing to customers in family packs through retailers significant business model innovation for Marico, which involved extending and cultivating the retailer channel for deeper and wider customer reach.

Making regular trips to untapped cities and the hinterland of western India, Harsh expanded the channel network to cover dealers who could stock family-size packs of Parachute oil and sell to customers. The result was significantly increased sales and higher market share for Parachute. A success-related 'problem' that emerged was the need to recruit sales and supervisory staff to serve the increasing demand. Harsh worked to strengthen his sales and distribution staff and reap the benefits of his marketing initiatives. Young at heart and in body, Harsh admits that the act of appointing new dealers in the interiors to sell the smaller tins to customers and booking their orders in the company registers gave him a high!

Harsh's initiative of introducing smaller 'family size' tins that contributed to higher sales was his first experiment in his pursuit of branding—to reach the customer directly in company packing. This success encouraged him to think bigger.

Now that end-users were the customers and the retail shelf was the point of contact, the container had to catch the eye of the beholder. This step demanded Parachute and Saffola to stand out from other items jostling for shelf space. He, thus, set his sights on changing the packaging from ungainly, tin containers to eye-catching plastic bottles.

Harsh was poised to create history in BOIL by the act of creating a brand out of a commodity.

Parachute's Packaging Makeover: As an offshoot of discovering the repackaging methods resorted to by retailers to meet end-user needs for 'small' quantities, Harsh was struck by the impact of packaging consumer products for retail shelves. While packaging was meant to protect the product, Harsh saw that it also influenced customer perception and boosted sales. He assessed that the smaller tin containers used to sell Parachute oil lacked visual appeal. Instead, attractively shaped and coloured plastic bottles attracted consumer attention.

Harsh recruited a packaging expert to implement the switchover from tin to plastic, which was lighter, cheaper and more attractive—all features being consumer friendly. However, while the trade involved in selling and stocking consumer oils had accepted the smaller tin packs, it resisted the transition to plastic. Despite evidence on positive consumer response, traders were not willing to accept plastic containers based on their past experience with suppliers of edible oil in plastic containers.

Harsh dug into their objections and traced the disaffection to rats chewing the square-shaped plastic containers, which provided the rodents a grip for biting into the plastic. This damage caused the oil to leak, resulting in dealers having to bear losses. To come up with practical solutions, Harsh presented this feedback to his R&D team, which worked with the vendors and designed the packaging as a cylindrical bottle. To get dealers to overcome their 'once bitten, twice shy' mentality, an experiment was conducted with a few rats rounded up in a cage along with some round plastic bottles. The dealers observed literally that the 'proof of the pudding was not in the eating' and no longer opposed the transition. Relatively expensive R&D technology ensured that the cap was leak-proof.

The packaging makeover did wonders to the perception of Parachute as a contemporary, premium oil. Retail and consumers now readily accepted Parachute oil in 500 millilitre plastic bottles. Subsequent introduction of the mini bottle pack converted the undecided 'loose oil users' to Parachute too. The field force was tasked with monitoring the conversion rate with dealers who were incentivized for achieving targets. As 'seeing is believing,' dealers' attitude changed with increasing consumer acceptance. The transformation was completed over the decade. Moreover, plastic being cheaper than tin, packaging costs came down. For BOIL, while the top line increased through volume and value, the bottom line went up in sync and market share rose significantly. Getting a conduit to link directly with customers and enabling them to buy Parachute oil in plastic packaging was the tipping point for branding. Advertising Parachute's value proposition while maintaining superior quality capped the ambitious branding exercise.

Products Become Brands: For BOIL's consumer products division, sustained business success required continued growth of end users—the number of customers purchasing Parachute coconut oil—which could happen only when customers perceived Parachute to be the best option to fulfil their needs. It was the marketer's job to assure customers that it was worth paying the premium for the superior benefits derived by using the product, given its convenient reach through effective distribution.

Harsh had realized that in contrast to the diluted brand image of Parachute, perceived more as a quality product than as a differentiated brand, the products of multinational corporations (MNCs) like Colgate and Hindustan Lever were perceived as brands available with compelling value proposition. There was a need to generate customer pull towards Marico brands. Thanks to the marketing knowledge obtained from his earnest pursuit of books, seminars and consultants besides his extensive field visits, Harsh had grasped the dynamics of FMCG branding.

For the maiden national advertising campaign, the advertising agency, faced with the challenge of projecting a common image of Parachute, adopted a pan-India value proposition based on the well-accepted virtues of the oil— its purity, clarity, aroma and the Indian tradition of using coconut oil.

GOOD FOR YOUR HEART

Harsh also worked on BOIL's other consumer brand, Saffola, which so far was retailed locally and in a couple of metro cities without any marketing fanfare. He commissioned a market research study, which revealed that safflower oil reduced cholesterol levels, a benefit endorsed by doctors. This revelation offered a unique differentiation opportunity for Saffola and this attribute was leveraged to attract customer attention. Harsh worked with the advertising agency and Saffola was launched as a healthy cooking oil. Positioned explicitly as being 'good for your heart', Saffola grabbed consumer attention with its dramatic communication. Clarion Advertising launched the brand and the early ads created a rather terrifying scenario of a man being wheeled into a hospital on a stretcher with the wailing of ambulance sirens in the background and a distressed wife looking on, seeking to reinforce the message that food cooked in Saffola could save your life—and your family.[8]

Choosing the health platform to promote an edible oil was a first by any company in the country. From a situation of casual demand for a safflower-based oil, a growing, health-conscious customer segment was created for Saffola. Through sustained efforts, Saffola's unique health benefits were promoted, with emphasis on doctor detailing. This enabled Saffola to differentiate itself from competition and reap a premium from customers. Harsh thus created, in the hitherto unbranded edible oil market that was largely retailed loose, a brand based on a compelling value proposition.

---

[8]Economic Times, 'Then & now: Saffola's communication shift over the years'. Available at: https://economictimes.indiatimes.com/then-now-saffolascommunication-shift-over-the-years/articleshow/11526735.cms

PASSION FOR MARKETING

Was it a gamble or an insight that drove Harsh to bet big on Parachute oil despite the cautious views of FMCG-tracking analysts? He was aware that the use of coconut oil was an age-old Indian practice. He bet on the insight that MNCs had not entered the coconut oil market and more importantly, were unlikely to do so given that this product was not featured in their global portfolio! This insight was backed by field knowledge that, within the country, use of coconut oil was nowhere near saturation. Moreover, user feedback indicated that coconut oil gelled well with the consumer trend to patronize branded products. In fact, Parachute in a plastic packaging had become a brand in its own right, popular enough to spawn fakes by the dozen! A new mould, expensive enough to deter copycats, prevented the situation from becoming an epidemic.

Harsh's pioneering consumer-directed innovations—from going small in family packs, leading the packaging transition from tin to tamper-proof, attractive plastic containers, and upgrading to pilfer-proof bottle caps, to advertising Parachute and Saffola as brands—were game changers originating from his strong belief in the differentiated value proposition of his products that could be leveraged to derive sustained, profitable growth.

These innovations differentiated Parachute and Saffola from the competition and helped these brands achieve dominant market share in their respective categories. It also reinforced the shift from a 'me too' commodity to a stand-out brand that commanded higher revenues, margins and growth rate. Besides driving the marketing strategy, Harsh instituted other key changes too. He brought in productivity enhancements in the plant, and put in place a 'first of its kind' comprehensive management information system (MIS)—a first for the FMCG industry then—to keep track of business data in real time. In the HR area, he introduced far-sighted policies and practices.

Enthused by the positive results achieved from his efforts, Harsh was able to patiently persuade his family to view what they perceived to be overheads as enablers of profitable growth for the company. With consent from the family management, customer-size packs were supplied to retailers in one state followed by another, assessing the consequences and outcomes of the action first before expanding to the next state. Harsh was happy to go along with this calculated approach as it enabled him to take his family along at every step.

The BOIL management's firm belief in incrementalism as the path to growth while avoiding risk, took the company eight years to make the full conversion from tin to plastic and for the nationwide expansion of the channel network. For Harsh, these were important make-or-break decisions to create a brand for which he was willing to make the trade-off between speed and family consent till the take-off stage. But was there a way to manage both effectively for accelerated growth? Harsh found a way to do so.

RESTRUCTURING BUSINESS

Over the years, by dint of his perseverance and efforts, Harsh had achieved sustainable results and managed to establish his credentials with the family as an accomplished marketer. Transitioning from treating consumer products as commodities to valuing them as consumer brands had a sustainable impact on revenues and margins for BOIL. The consumer products business had, by the 1980s, outpaced the chemicals and spice-extract business divisions of BOIL. With the gradual introduction of consumer-size packs in plastic and brand-based-marketing, revenues of the consumer products division had more than doubled every five years.

Harsh was keen to extend the portfolio of both brands in BOIL's consumer products division, which was the cash cow and could grow to be BOIL's raison d'être. However, Harsh could perceive some speed breakers obstructing the enormous potential of this division. He realized that the traditional, conservative, family-managed style of unhurried decision-making based on a moderate approach to growth was suboptimal for accelerated growth of the consumer products division. Successfully operating a branded consumer product business required an attitude and skill set different from those needed to manage the steadily growing B2B commodity divisions of BOIL.

There was an urgent need to change the conventional family business style of running the enterprise in a way that would not make the BOIL management uncomfortable. Harsh became increasingly conscious of this need for change. He understood that when family businesses grow beyond a 'point', its owners have to make a difficult decision: to either professionalize or to keep the status quo by focusing on the day-to-day management of the business.

Seeking a harmonious solution, he sourced information

on similar situations prevailing globally and exchanged experiences with his friends—fellow CEOs of family businesses in India. Also, guidance from his mentor Professor Ram Charan, a reputed global business strategist and advisor to CEOs, was crucial at this stage. It became clear to Harsh that the solution was to operate the consumer product business as an independent entity. Harsh had to put across this solution in a manner that was acceptable to the family.

To do this, Harsh started by pointing out the benefits of specialization for each division. Marketing was the determinant factor for consumer products. Chemicals required a technology bias. Spice extracts was an export-oriented trading business. There was no synergy in the way each business operated. Hence, the better approach would be to run each business as a separate entity. Actually, the fourth-generation Mariwalas had already divided the company's business lines among themselves informally. With persuasion and conviction, Harsh was able to have his proposal accepted and in the year 1981, the consumer products business was hived off as a separate profit centre. It became one of the four profit centres of BOIL.

This arrangement seemed to be a major makeover in the management of the Group. Separating the divisions bestowed greater authority to the heads. However, it soon became evident that this was a halfway solution. Crucial financial decisions like those relating to deployment of profits were still made subjectively. The consumer products division continued to be treated as the cash cow for other businesses. Inevitably, gross under-investment in production facilities to serve increasing demand forced the consumer products division to outsource manufacturing, affecting product quality in the absence of manufacturers with standard processes. Worse, the newly created consumer product division continued to be perceived externally as a family-managed business, which meant it could not attract the talent essential for business growth in the FMCG sector, despite Harsh's best efforts to manage Parachute and Saffola as branded consumer products.

The talent gap led to a number of product launch failures in the late 1980s, which saw an explosion of brands in the market for refined sunflower oil. When Hindustan Lever and ITC Agritech launched Flora and Sundrop edible oils, respectively, BOIL too introduced its brand, Sweekar, in a market that had become competitive. It followed with other products like Parachute's filtered groundnut oil and Parachute's packaged pulses. However, notwithstanding the success of brand Parachute, these brand extensions were failures due to weak market research and superficial analysis, besides inadequate operational processes and systems. Harsh realized that the failure caused by inadequate insights on competition and customers was consummated by inflated 'premium' pricing.

Further, just as the business had grown, so had the number of family members involved in the management of this enterprise. So, even though Harsh and his cousins running the other profit centres were not interested in the business of their counterparts, being perceived as a large family-managed business group was a major stumbling block to induct professional management, crucial for the consumer products group at this accelerated growth stage. By the late 1980s, there were nine Mariwala cousins in BOIL, compounding the challenge of recruiting professionals for the consumer products division. It became clear to Harsh that the existing state of affairs at BOIL inhibited the growth of the consumer products business. At this stage, of growth what the business required was less family and more professionals to man the organization. He was clear that it was now time grant autonomy of operations to the different businesses of BOIL for unhindered growth. Summing up, the consumer products division had attained adulthood and required funding and professional talent for rapid, not incremental, scaling up, as was the case with the other business divisions, both of which were not possible in the present set-up. Also, the family was apprehensive of acquiring talent at market-based terms. Making matters more complex was the reality of each Mariwala having due authority in the business, but with no accountability. In Harsh's words: 'It was clear that I had to let go of the old style of working. The days of Bombay Oil Industries were over. When I think of what happened with R.V. Bindhumadhavan, our packaging head, I still cringe. One general manager of BOIL asked him, "So you have come here to buy dabba baatli (boxes and bottles)?"[9] Bindhumadhavan was a packaging expert from Ranbaxy who had recently been recruited for the Consumer Products division.

To squarely face these complex issues, Harsh assembled his cousins involved in running BOIL. At the end of the

---

[9]Krishna Gopalan, 'Harsh Mariwala's diary note', *Outlook Business*, Collector's Edition, 26 March 2018. Available at: https://www.outlookbusiness.com/specials/secret-diary-of-an-entrepreneur_2018/in-the-fmcg-business-it-is-alwayssmall-innovations-driven-by-common-sense-that-have-made-thedifference-4355

discussions, in Harsh's words, 'We all agreed that we did not see eye-to-eye in the matters of running the business. Plus there were no synergies in the businesses of Bombay Oil, so we wondered about the point of being together.'[10]

BREAKING FREE

Leveraging his seniority, Harsh marshalled the cousins for a now-or-never 'round table' to sensitize them on the unintended consequences of how BOIL was being run and to forge an agreement in the best interests of BOIL as a group, to optimize the interest of each family CEO.

The cousins agreed, but family discussions on the division of assets were not always smooth and often intense. Negotiations between Harsh and 'the others' ebbed and flowed on the issues of control of assets and decisions on finance for capital expenditure. Setbacks notwithstanding, Harsh persisted doggedly as he had the most to lose—and gain. He recounts, 'Separation is never easy. Even the smallest issues had to be discussed threadbare.'

Eventually, the family worked out a solution, devised among themselves, that proactively pre-empted external recourse or a family break-up. This solution was to morph the various businesses into autonomous subsidiaries with BOIL as the holding company owning the assets, including the brands that would continue to generate royalty for BOIL. Each subsidiary company would be headed by one branch of the Mariwala family with the roles and responsibilities laid

---

[10]Sonu Bhasin, *The Inheritors: Stories of Entrepreneurship and Success,* Portfolio, Chapter 2, 2017.

out in a comprehensive family charter prepared to ensure a trouble-free growth of the group companies. All investment decisions were to be taken with the consent of the holding company.

Eventually, in 1990, the consumer products division became Marico Industries. Epro Bio-Technologies was established to make hybrid seeds; the spice extracts division was spun off as a separate subsidiary called Kancor Flavours and Extracts Ltd; and the chemical division was merged with Hindustan Polyamides and Fibres, a Pune-based firm acquired by BOIL. The holding company also retained the ownership of Parachute and Saffola brands and earned royalties until year 2000, when Marico purchased the brand rights from BOIL for ₹30 crore. By then the revenues of the consumer products division had grown to almost 80 per cent of BOIL's revenue—from ₹50 lakh in 1971 to ₹80 crore out of BOIL's total turnover of ₹102 crore in 1990.

Harsh's profound learnings over two decades since his internship in the field and coaching by his network of mentors and experts, had stood him in good stead in steering the way forward for BOIL's consumer products division. The innovative breakthroughs in branding and brand extensions, besides extending channel reach, had highlighted the compelling value proposition of these brands, fetching premium pricing multiplied by increasing sales. Underpinning the learning experiences was the reality of developing a professional environment to attract talent for achieving scope and scale in business.

Does Harsh regret that he joined the family business as an ordinary commerce graduate? Could he have achieved what he did in less time? In retrospect, Harsh has no regrets. Had he joined BOIL after attending a business school and armed with sophisticated notions of corporate management, he would have immediately run into conflict with his family. With no pretentions of management knowledge, Harsh learnt the basics of running a business from the ground up. For him, the experience of acquiring the know-how of branding and growing a consumer product business in India from scratch—through the grind of rejuvenating the trade channel, innovating packaging, unveiling the enormous potential of brands Parachute and Saffola and creating a merit-cum-value-based organization from first principles was more valuable than acquiring a post-graduate degree in management from anywhere. The icing on the cake was developing the ability to exercise deep patience with family members' unresponsive attitude towards change, and the perseverance to bring them in line with his vision for Marico. He practised learning through failing without the debilitating fear of failure.

As he says, 'I had to learn the business virtually by the seat-of-my-pants, which gave me first-hand knowledge of how traditional Indian businesses are run. The change in thinking and approach, as it evolved over 15 years, came in small incremental steps hardly perceivable as it happened. I realized that if I had to influence the change process, I had to live with two opposing realities of tradition and contemporariness until time would make these realities converge.' That was when Harsh achieved the consensus on hiving off the consumer products division as a separate entity, Marico. For him, breaking away from the family or even BOIL was never an option. The emotional burden of severing relations with a family that had grown the business over three generations would be too much to bear. That was just not the Harsh Mariwala way!

As a medium-sized enterprise, a growth-oriented Marico was now poised to take its place in the league of large FMCG companies. Incidentally, by then, the socioeconomic environment in India had evolved significantly over the decades since Independence. These changes had a profound impact on new-age consumers and on the FMCG industry, especially Mariwala's Marico.

Let us see how Harsh and his top management team (TMT) shaped Marico over the next stage of the enterprise's life cycle in an era marked by changing consumer behaviour for FMCGs.

Chapter 4

Shaping Marico

Harsh now had a clear vision of the way forward for Marico, his own entrepreneurial venture and the erstwhile consumer products division of BOIL, while adhering to the Family Charter. Not just as a seller of edible and coconut oil—but as an authentic Indian consumer brands company, striving to make its place among major FMCG companies, including multinational entities in India and the emerging markets—and acknowledged as much for corporate governance as for consumer relevance. With uncommon sense that served as the springboard for a place in the sun, this national FMCG player spread its wings in an India that was emerging from the restrictive mindset of the past. It was the beginning of the new decade before the millennium, and branding trends in consumer India were becoming innovative, thanks to the rising influence of the younger generation.

WINDS OF LIBERALIZATION

Marico was born against the backdrop of the country welcoming some sweeping economic reforms, initiated in the late 1980s and continued in the early 1990s, which brought in its wake higher GDP growth rate and rise in the purchasing power of rural households too. The country was breathing the elixir of rising standards in living. This set the ball rolling for the long-stalled consumer products industry. The pent-up demand for choice and availability was matched by the latent managerial ability to scope and scale—ironically, thanks in good measure to investments in quality higher education made during the socialist era!

Indian industry too availed of the opportunity to achieve economies of scope and scale, ensuring affordability and reach for consumer products, an industry in which multinationals had established a firm market-hold, due to their distribution reach and international marketing experience.

Expanding demand and supply dynamics was the dominant characteristic of the period following the dismantling of licences, permits and controls. From cigarettes to snacks, deodorants to pencils, skin creams to what have you, Indian enterprises, micro, small, medium, large and mega, engaged in making and marketing products tailored for the long-suppressed needs of the customer, accessible through India's myriad outlets ranging from single person, to hole-in-the wall outlets or paan shops, to general kirana shops and department stores.

Consumer products and retail are intimately linked. In developed countries, thanks to the concentration of trade, prevalence of modern retail and emergence of e-commerce, the number of retail outlets per thousand of population has come down. In India however, the reverse is true, this statistic has increased. With improved infrastructure, including better logistics, most of rural India has come within the network of retail. To complement enhanced reach, rise in rural income and greater awareness through television and other media were the key ingredients in the recipe for increasing rural consumption. Another retail statistic relevant to India—during the late 1960s, three lakh retail outlets sold branded products to India's population of 550 million. Compare this with today's population of 1.2 billion served by an estimated 12 million outlets in both the organized and unorganized sectors!

New-Age FMCG: The evolution of the consumer products sector witnessed some welcome value innovations. In 1990, Nirma was a newly launched detergent powder that blazed a trail for serving the mass market with a 'Made in India' value-for-money product. Entrepreneur Karsanbhai, hailing from a 'common family', hit the jackpot with the right 'price–value' benefit combination, conveyed vividly through a catchy jingle, which urged a switchover from soap bars. It was a breakthrough example of expanding the market by offering value, winning first-time users and weaning customers from unbranded competitors.

Another typically Indian, frugal innovation was the introduction of the sachet pack as the single serve for one-time use or consumption, or trial. The critical element of the value chain was last-mile accessibility—the 'cubby hole' of a shop stocking an assortment of items like paan, loose cigarettes, bread, eggs or snacks, which combined affordability with the highest ease of transaction for an emerging, aspiring India. Sachets were the single big innovation to reach first-time users and expand market share for a wide range of branded consumer products in urban and rural India.

Customizing Brand Strategy: As MNCs like HUL and others have realized and come to terms with, India is not a homogenous market for consumer products. For instance, HUL realized that even for coffee, a beverage traditionally identified with the South, filter coffee is the preferred coffee in Tamil Nadu while people in Karnataka have a different taste profile. HUL thus launched a lighter version of its coffee brand Bru, specifically for the Karnataka market. Marico too realized that embracing the finer nuances around local tastes was important to build brand strategy, thereby successfully elevating Parachute coconut oil from the category of a home commodity to a sought-after name and a national brand for pure, clear, coconut oil with aroma.

FMCG Career by Choice: The 1990s brought about freedom from controls and taboos on what was earlier termed as 'conspicuous consumption' like travelling abroad, owning a car or even enjoying a Coke. India's surging GDP growth rate post the restrictive licence-permit-control era, brought about a mindset change in Indians, especially graduating students of elite educational institutions. To them, liberalization meant pursuing new career aspirations. Selection to the coveted Indian Administrative Service was no longer the mecca of all career destinations as it was during the socialist period. Many were lured to acquire an MBA qualification for a well-paid career in the corporate world, especially in the consumer products sector. These FMCG companies, MNCs and their national counterparts, attracted attention with innovative packages that were enticing. While the public sector provided security and 'stolidity', these corporates beckoned with responsibility and rupees. Faced with such career propositions, the preference of the Now Generation was clearly glamour and gains.

Marico too was able to position itself as a sought-after placement option for MBA graduates from top B-Schools. Domestic corporates with a professional outlook could afford such packages, mostly from the value created through branding, unlike typical small business owners who perceived packaging and branding as unnecessary additions to cost, rather than enhancement of value. Attuned to the jugaad mindset of doing business, packaging had to be functionally adequate and branding was taken to mean 'naamkaran,' or naming.

For the lala or local small business owner, value was the margin the company eked out after keeping the price low as demanded by the market and adding up costs as demanded by the suppliers and labour, as well as to recover overheads. When the efforts to be competitive are based on time-honoured methods of reducing cost, the game is to play one supplier against another, adopt quality measures only as mandated and recruit staff from the community. Few Indian companies had the know-all and gall to successfully deploy marketing as strategy till liberalization made it feasible. The environment was till then conducive to engage in full-fledged marketing as licences, permits and capacity controls restricted pricing and scaling.

This was the backdrop against which the Indian consumer product sector was rapidly changing and Mariwala was setting the pace on his own journey with Marico, the karmabhoomi of his experiments with shaping a business institution. It was time to articulate his dream of becoming one among the top consumer product companies in the country, not deterred by the reality that presently the company sold all of two branded consumer products—an edible oil and a coconut oil. Harsh was poised for change—to take the leap into the future.

EMERGING FROM THE COCOON

Marico was in the making from the late 1980s. For Harsh, infected by Professor Bhandari's missionary belief that anything 'touched' by the customer was 'brand-worthy', the 'future was Marico's to make'. The task at hand was to build the foundation for a professionally managed, growth-driven, Indian consumer products company known for its brands.

Harsh had to make Marico emerge from the remains of a modest consumer product division of an unassuming, old-world company, even while pushing for accelerated growth. This meant developing existing brands, introducing portfolio additions and business expansion on the one hand and building an organization that functioned on merit and transparency, pursuing a 'win or learn' attitude to handle the risk of failure on the other hand. For business expansion, it was necessary to get Marico ready for a public issue. These were objectives the family would never have considered. Now as managing director (MD) of Marico, Harsh focused on bringing in the talent, piloting product innovation and launching new products.

As Mariwala puts it, 'The 1990s were particularly stressful. The decision to set up Marico meant that I was working 18 hours a day. Hiring the team and getting things working took up most of my time.'

Talent Team: Harsh believed that growth for any institution starts at the top. When the top management has a growth mindset, the company grows. As Harsh states, 'I believe we have to go on growing the top line and automatically the bottom line will come. This was a big challenge.'

Harsh had inherited about 200 employees from BOIL but needed to attract fresh talent to build Marico's brands. He initiated efforts to put together his TMT starting with onboarding an experienced HR professional. However, unable to afford mass advertising, Harsh hit upon an innovative approach to rouse nationwide interest in Marico's arrival and intention to recruit 'can do' talent.

A striking media campaign with two banner headlines '*200 Employees Walk Out of Bombay Oil*' and '*Mass Killer Nabbed*' was launched,[11] heralding the arrival of a 'happening' company with reputed brands, arousing interest among management professionals to check the credentials of the company. This was followed up by interactions at top B-Schools that triggered interest among recruits-to-be to start their career in an ambitious consumer products organization-in-the-making. The talent acquisition initiative included a team of scientists and technical experts to man the new laboratory commissioned at Jalgaon in 1993–94 to prototype brand extensions for Parachute and Saffola and subsequently

---

[11]Wealthy Matters, 'Harsh Mariwala on His Family Business', 15 July 2012. Available at: https://wealthymatters.com/2012/07/15/harsh-mariwala-on-his-familybusiness/

for new products too. The highly visible campaign worked—Marico was able to draw the talent it was looking for, marking an auspicious start for the venture!

Mission and Values: Creating an organization filled with high-performance managers from various organizations and cultures was one thing, but melding and retaining them as performing Mariconians was quite another! A Mission and Values document for Mariconians was, therefore, created to help them identify with what was the need of the hour for the fledgling company.

Harsh and his team prepared a working draft of the document for adoption, after discussions with the next-level senior management team, all of whom had joined Marico with the common desire of growing a new consumer product venture. Mariwala's passion and keenness to jointly build the business was the glue that bound them together. And together they gave final shape to the Corporate Mission and Values document for Marico. To foster a sense of family, Marico chose to refer to every employee as a 'member'.

Was this exercise different from similar events conducted in the corporate world—in getaway resorts? The difference between precept and practice is seen in walking the talk. In Mariwala's words, 'In any culture-building journey of an organization, the role of the middle and top management is crucial. If someone takes it lightly and says "this is the managing director's values," then those values will just not percolate throughout the organization.' Mariwala led by walking the talk, and by clarifying the what, who and why of the company.

Marico's mission statement packaged its vision, business goals and philosophy. It described itself as a consumer-oriented enterprise operating in a highly competitive sector delivering superior-quality FMCG products to satisfy household needs while being constantly innovative. Marico perceived itself as a differentiated, flexible and growing organization, as well as a responsible corporate citizen at the top of its chosen business lines, generating optimal profits.

Marico's value statement was a guide to its members' actions on how to behave in the everyday conduct of business. It was woven around the three Ps of People, Products and Profits. It envisaged that its people would invest in sustainable relationships with customers, business partners and organization members; its products would generate and sustain customer loyalty; and its profits, essential for reinvestment in expanding the market, were a source of wealth maximization for all stakeholders. While Marico's Mission reflects its clarity and conviction in spelling out what it will pursue and be known for, its Values define its accountability to its stakeholders.

Marico had a full team of qualified junior to top management in place, and the management collective comprising the top three of the five rungs in Marico's hierarchy, disseminated the mission and values among other organizational members. Mariconians were one with the Mission and Values they had collectively constructed. The organizational mindset was geared to drive Marico as an emerging FMCG enterprise, energized for escalating growth.

Birthday resolutions are meant for the day, but Harsh was clear that Marico's birthday resolution was meant for every day. At Marico, being conscious of the 3P values started on recruitment day, and then absorbing them and displaying them in practice forged the way ahead. As Mariwala states, 'We were done with the old ways of working. Marico had to forge a new growth culture.'[12] He was clear that growth was the tonic for healthy survival and for attracting and retaining talent. Also, chasing growth was acceptable so long as it was profitable and the growth curve was secular, even though initially, margins could be impacted adversely. The organization, thus, set for itself a fifth-year target goal of ₹300 crore in its first Strategic Business Plan for the period 1991–96 with a new product to be added to its portfolio every year.[13] Achieving this goal would be the spring board to yank Marico from the clutches of mediocrity as an SME.

REPOSITIONING BRANDS

Harsh was conscious that Marico was now a branded consumer products company with an inspiring mission, a fresh, charged, talented team and two successful brands, operating on its own steam in a competitive environment.

Retail and consumers now readily accepted Parachute oil in 500 millilitre plastic bottles. The subsequent introduction of the mini bottle pack helped to convert the undecided 'loose oil users' to Parachute too. Having set the trend in packaging

---

[12]Krishna Gopalan, 'Harsh Mariwala's Diary Note', *Outlook Business*, 26 March 2018. Available at: https://www.outlookbusiness.com/specials/secret-diary-of-anentrepreneur_2018/in-the-fmcg-business-it-is-always-small-innovationsdriven-by-common-sense-that-have-made-the-difference-4355
[13]S.B. Budhiraja and M.B. Athreya, *Cases in Strategic Management*, Tata McGraw Hill, p.74

innovation, with lighter plastic containers for Parachute and Saffola oils in the mid-1980s, Marico introduced sachet packs to induce semi-urban and rural users of coconut oil to make the switch to Parachute. These sachet packs were distributed to incentivize new dealers, promoted as giveaways at rural events like haats, or markets, and through local advertising. By then Harsh's sales staff had extended Marico's reach into India's hinterland. The measures came at a cost but were successful in expanding the customer base sustainably and significantly. Marico, thus, focused on building its prized asset of loyal customers. These pioneering marketing innovations for a mundane product like coconut oil saw sales zoom for Parachute. The market opened up for Parachute as Marico went rural in a big way. Harsh observed that the impact of expanding distribution and spending money on promotions led to repeat customer sales—the sachets had done their job—and increasing offtake from dealers. To meet the growing demand from brand growth, Marico established a new plant in Palghat district of Kerala to manufacture Parachute coconut oil with a capacity of 24,000 tonnes of coconut oil per annum, which began commercial operation in May 1993.

By the mid-1990s a new generation was coming of age in the country. Marico commissioned a qualitative study on what Parachute stood for in the mind of the millennial generation. This study reiterated that Parachute as a brand stood for purity, nourishment and heritage. However, it was not found to be associated with liveliness and youthfulness, attributes relevant to the 'now' generation. These perceptions spotted by the study were useful to identify brand extensions for Parachute and resulted in some new products like Parachute Advansed and Parachute Jasmine hair oil.

Marico designed a modern logo for the Parachute Advansed and Parachute Jasmine oil bottles. The bottles got a facelift with a contemporary look to its shape and to the pack graphics. Would this bright and lively change help catch the attention of the youth? Happily, for the Marico team, Parachute's brand extensions met with success. It was an opportune time for Marico to view its present, limited brands as the core of an expanding portfolio of personal products to serve the emerging needs of the new generation.

Marico also commissioned a creative consultant to conduct a consumer insight study on brand Saffola. The outcome of the study was to reposition Saffola from a restricted, curative heart platform to a larger 'heart of a healthy family' platform, enabling brand extensions in the 'healthy foods for the family', category. From a single brand for 30 years, Saffola has since spawned five brand extensions with more in the pipeline. For instance, Marico launched Saffola Masala Oats as a brand extension, which was originally positioned as breakfast food, but subsequently as an in-between meal or snack. The brand extension carved a niche for itself and dominates it. Marico also extended the reach of its refined sunflower oil, Sweekar, nationally in 1991.

In the two years following its birth, Marico doubled revenues from ₹80 crore to ₹159 crore. For the first time, Marico's oil business was operating within a five-year business plan with a well-crafted marketing strategy and budget for execution. The budget earmarked expenditure for recruitment and deployment of Marico sales force in the field, widespread advertising and product promotion and investment in plant and machinery to cater to the projected growth in demand. As anticipated in the business plan, the revenues grew and surpassed the target of ₹300 crore while margins halved from an average of 8 per cent in the previous three years to 4 per cent—a clear example of Mariwala's growth mindset. As you reap, so you sow. Thereafter, the company has managed to stay above industry growth rates in both revenues and operating margins.

Yet, Marico had goals to achieve and risks to take. Harsh understood that innovation was needed to drive Marico's growth, which meant experimentation within affordable limits. For doing this, Harsh could rely on his talent team. He devoted attention to building an HR organization equipped to handle this ambitious task.

EMPOWERMENT FOR INNOVATION

Harsh instituted belief in the 'you succeed or you learn' attitude to defang the 'fear of failure' in the company. This meant when the loss was affordable, the failure, if at all, would only lead to learning. Creating a positive attitude towards experimentation set the mindset for innovation.

Mariwala's attitude toward failure has a parallel with Intel CEO Andy Grove's Objective and Key Results (OKR) approach to institutionalize innovation. Grove developed this OKR philosophy in the 1970s as an alternative to the then popular Management by Objectives mantra. The OKR system is more open to acceptance of failure and promotes setting aspirational goals every quarter, which can be achieved by means that are transparent and verifiable. This is contrary to the Management by Objectives system that promotes setting up annual goals. Marico's outlook towards its employees and work is similar to the philosophy underlying the OKR approach to people management, which became popular from the late 1970s. It's Employment Value Proposition, the talent differentiator for the company, believes in motivating members to innovate in the spirit of 'you succeed or you learn'. This belief when practised diligently, dissolves the 'fear of failure' barrier holding back innovative behaviour.

Mariwala understood that one could not command human qualities like creativity, passion and initiative in an organization, as these attributes are what people choose to bring to work every day—or not. What Marico had to therefore institute was 'a work culture where risk taking for experimenting was encouraged and failure was not punished, if it was an intelligent error, which made Marico an innovation-driven organization.' A growth mindset is the breeding ground for innovation, and this was infused in the attitude of Mariconians by the top management. This in turn, created a culture that promoted values, trust, merit, transparency and empowerment that together embraced innovation at work.

Work Innovation: Marico, an organization with just five levels, developed an open culture promoting access across functions, with people addressing each other informally on first name basis and speaking to each other across ranks in an environment of trust. With few rules for attendance, leaves or reimbursement, Mariconians delivered high compliance. No clemency was spared for trust violators. Marico also promoted diversity among its members, extending beyond gender and geography. This brought forth new perspectives in discussions. Harsh and his TMT set an example of walking the talk in living the company culture.

Product Innovation: As a branded consumer product company, Marico had a valued place for technologists, scientists and specialists in consumer insighting to ensure continuous brand relevance. Marico believed that success in new product development depended on the efficacy of the consumer insighting process as it identified emerging consumer trends and helped translate them into need, satisfying products, whether as brand extensions or portfolio expansions. Marico's research team developed product prototypes to test for a hypothesis-product-market fit, while adopting a low-cost, fail-fast model. Thereafter, the decision to scale was taken. Over time, Marico brands ranked within the top two or three in over 90 per cent of the product categories and subcategories in which they figured.

Marico's modern, well-equipped laboratory in Mumbai was manned by a team of formulation chemists, nutritionists and packaging technologists. Manufacturing was streamlined and upgraded for quality, volume and operational efficiency. To maintain the pipeline of new product introduction and brand extensions, around 15 per cent of annual profits were earmarked for product innovation in the domain of beauty and wellness.

The first new product launch from Marico was a non-sticky hair oil under the brand name Hair & Care. The brand was a success, as much due to the sleek, transparent, plastic pack as to the vitamin E packed in the product. This was a well-timed introduction as demand for non-stick hair oil in a millennial market was growing faster than for traditional hair oil. However, not all new product launches met with absolute success.

Between 1992 and 1994, the company had a mixed record with new product introductions. Former Marico employee Vikas Verma, among the first set of management recruits in 1991, narrates, 'Harsh would come back from his travels and throw at us a new product idea that he found in the stores abroad.' One such was a fabric starch spray that eventually spawned Revive, the fabric care brand. It is a cold water starch that makes starching of cottons more convenient for the consumer. It was an R&D triumph for Marico, an innovation that created a new product category by tapping a long-unmet customer need. Despite a price premium of 40 per cent over local brands, the superior value proposition of Revive made it an instant success.

Process Innovation: Innovation at Marico extended beyond the product to innovations in business processes, including in-house manufacturing to outsourcing, adding online distribution, acquisition of start-ups and in business model process diverting emphasis from B2B to B2C.

In fact, Marico became the first FMCG company in India to integrate distributor sales and stock information with the company's own Management Information System for sales and stocks. This meant that changes in sales and stock figures of every distributor and retailer were available with the company in 'real time', that is on per-transaction basis. Using Artificial Intelligence and data analytics, Marico could reasonably forecast the sales and stock levels of a distributor and ensure that cases of stock pile-up and stock-out situations were negligible in the system. The system generated the recommended stock keeping unit (SKU) levels for every distributor and retailer. The installation of the integrated MIS resulted in significant improvements in servicing customers as both the company and the retailer were now able to monitor sales and inventory movements in real time, with no time lag in the updation of data. Intelligently automating the system led to freeing up more than 1,100 man-days in the value chain, by company estimates in terms of manpower reduction, primarily in warehousing and sales administration jobs and with distributors and dealers. This was a 'big bang' switch involving field sales staff, distributors, retailers and Marico's IT Centre, effectively cutting off 'escape buttons' that could hold back full implementation. This is characteristic of Marico's decisiveness in action after due diligence.

With this MIS in place, the time-honoured practice in the consumer products industry of pushing stocks at the month end, quarter end and year end became redundant in Marico. Buy-in from distributors for the software was obtained by making it distributor centric, which meant distributors could use the same software with Marico as well as with other principals' data. In contrast with consumer goods companies that added complication and exercised might, Marico's imaginative IT Systems focused on clarity of processes and trade equity, creating a competitive advantage for the company and channel members. Competition, big and bigger, took more than six years to catch up.

Next on the IT radar was the buying process of the key commodity for Marico—copra or dried coconut. Marico is the largest consumer of coconuts in the country, accounting for one in 13 coconuts produced. Marico has developed a long-term relationship with coconut farmers by setting up coconut collection centres in farming areas, thereby doing away with middlemen for mutual benefit. Marico took up the challenge of getting copra dealers who procured coconuts from farmers and processed them to form copra—an input for the oil refinery—on its portal for processing transactions, information on logistics and payments, all in real time. This resulted in speedier processing of information for demand forecasting, inventory and supplier management, yielding considerable cost savings. Why did the dealers cooperate? Because of Marico's fair trade practices and prompt payments, besides of course, being the largest buyer. The transformation could happen because of smooth coordination between the copra buying and IT teams enabling spot decisions to be taken, which reflects Marico's culture of merit and empowerment.

The IT department annually receives more than 600 suggestions from coconut farmers, copra dealers, procurement staff and IT department. These suggestions are assessed and the good ones implemented within a year, after due analysis for payback, which means the cost incurred in executing the suggestion should be recovered through savings realized within a year.

Marico also relied on new technology tools to drive its push into rural markets. To improve utilization of resources and cost-to-serve in rural van operations, Marico is using technology such as geo-tracking of van routes, which measures the distance travelled and time taken on every route between company warehouses and distributors, daily. 'This helps identify inefficient routes and re-deploy resources into high business potential routes continuously,' remarks Sanjay Mishra, COO, Marico. He adds that since these innovations, especially geo-tracking, the company has increased its direct distribution reach by 20 per cent, which means higher productivity of field staff, as the same number of field staff can effectively service distributors and retailers.

WORKER MANAGEMENT

Marico's management–worker relationship has withstood the test of time. By 1996, Marico had four manufacturing locations and a few dedicated third-party sources for its products to keep up with the growing pace of sales. Its Palakkad factory in the management–worker strife-stricken Kerala has had uninterrupted production to this day. To cultivate a relationship of trust and comradeship, workers were clubbed into four houses of Marico and sports events conducted after work, fostering friendly competition among them, and between them and the company; this helped to reinforce the feeling of membership. These matches also served to distract the workers from indulging in high 'spirit-ed' activity to while away idle time. This is truly a sustainable innovation in the HR area. Could this initiative have emerged from Harsh's learning in an earlier situation of confronting the headstrong trade union leader Datta Samant during a labour strike in BOIL in the 1980s that went on for more than a year without any willingness by either side to settle?

The branded FMCG company was gaining recognition for its innovative and enlightened practices in the People and Performance area. Marico's turnover in the fifth year of the Strategic Business Plan was ₹348 crore, as against the targeted figure of ₹300 crore! The company's business metrics were equally encouraging. Its portfolio of leadership brands had increased to six, all of which ranked within the top two in their respective market segments.

AN EMERGING MARKET MNC

Within six years from Marico's inception, Parachute and Saffola were well recognized nationally as quality consumer brands. Between 1992–94, Marico went from exporter to being a successful international marketer. Harsh, looking at multiple pillars of growth, felt it was time to make a foray into overseas markets. The first choice were locations with sizeable Indian diaspora familiar with Parachute and Saffola brands. In 1995, the company commenced its international business by setting up an office in Dubai that functioned as a single-point business promotion facility for Marico. Marketing functions like distribution, creating a dealer network, promotions and advertising, backed up by a field sales team created awareness and built up business. Gradually, the office extended its scope to cover the Middle East and Egypt. Initially, Marico's overseas operations were incubated separately by corporate marketing in Mumbai to disallow Marico brand managers to have 'escape buttons' for explaining away inaction. However, with the contribution of global business expanding to over

20 per cent of total turnover, international and domestic operations were combined.

Globally Marico operates in Bangladesh, the Middle East, Egypt and South Africa. It also has business offices in Indonesia, Malaysia and Thailand. In Bangladesh, Marico is the largest listed Indian MNC, and Parachute has a dominant market share of 80 per cent in coconut oil. Marico's presence in many countries is associated with local acquisitions of brands in the Beauty and Wellness category. Marico thus became an emerging market multinational, present in 25 African and Asian countries. Its global revenues accounted for 22 per cent of Marico's turnover in FY19.

FROM MISSION TO DIRECTION

Marico had reached its milestone for prolonged growth as a consumer products company. It was gaining recognition in the capital markets as a major professionally managed Indian consumer product entity. The company planned to go public but there was first a hurdle to be overcome. Marico needed a clear business direction.

Going public meant external accountability. So far, Marico's TMT was accountable to itself, which meant to the company's mission and values. Going public required greater clarity on the mission statement of Marico as a corporate entity. Interactions with analysts, issue managers, broking houses and financial institutions also unveiled unintended ambiguities in the strategic guidance for growth laid down in the Mission Statement.

Following a detailed review, it was felt that Marico had

reached the stage to substitute the Mission Statement with a Business Direction statement. In adopting this perspective, Harsh was much influenced by his mentor Professor Ram Charan, who believed more in setting a clear business direction than following a vision. Harsh was struck by his 80:20 rule, which allotted more time to direction. The underlying assumption of the 80:20 rule is that the business environment is subject to quick changes and requires more attention, while vision can be articulated based on setting the direction.

The basic business direction set for Marico in India was seeking opportunities through a presence in consumer products and markets, which other large corporations do not find interesting. In this scenario, Marico would be a pioneer and build on the first-mover advantage to sustainably grow the business, thanks to its competitive advantage in innovation and its empowered organization with aligned talent, making up for the financial clout of large corporations (MNCs). Globally, Marico would acquire or invest in consumer brands with dominant value propositions in emerging markets. For example, Marico acquired Code 10, a popular male grooming brand in Malaysia, to gain a foothold in the country. It also invested in Parachute Beliphool plant in Bangladesh to strengthen its presence. In India or abroad, the company's areas of strategic interest were Beauty and Wellness, domains wherein the company primarily operates. As a consequence of setting Business Direction, Marico was reorganized under the three businesses of Personal Care, Foods and International Business. These served as directions to Marico for identifying growth opportunities and planning for expansion in India and abroad, within the FMCG space.

In 1994, as per the terms of the Family Charter, Harsh and his youngest uncle, Kishore Mariwala, were required to buy out the shares of the two other uncles, for which they had to borrow funds at high interest. Marico, hence, planned an IPO with the twin objectives of raising money to sustain the accelerated pace of growth and for promoters to earn returns on their investment.

Taking a calculated risk as the current capital market outlook was not conducive for seeking fresh capital, Marico went public in 1996 at a relatively high premium of ₹165 on par value of ₹10 per share at 13 times multiple of the Price/Earnings ratio. As Mariwala states, 'In 1996, we bit the bullet and went public at ₹175 a share. I was so nervous.' Mariwala's burden lifted when the issue was subscribed twice over. Simultaneously, the two founders diluted their holding to the tune of 26.25 lakh equity shares at the price as per the terms of the IPO. The financial objectives of going public were more than adequately met. Marico was recognized as a family-owned, professionally driven, successful consumer product company.

However, coming in the public eye meant opening oneself to takeover threats, especially when India had opened up to multinationals and the market for FMCG, was growing handsomely.

BORN AGAIN, STRONGER

While liberalization was an inflexion point for the country, freeing the economy from a host of controls, it also paved the way for FMCG multinationals to expand operations in India through joint ventures, acquisitions and greenfield ventures. MNCs responded, with the clear intent of dominating the sector. In their trail came the Foreign Institutional Investors (FIIs) who brought in the concept of valuation for buying equity in Indian companies. This situation could potentially pose a life threat for local companies becoming takeover targets, particularly companies with a promising track record of fast growth and high brand acceptance—Marico being a good example in the mid-1990s. The 'big, bad wolf' of the multinational FMCG world was eyeing Marico, shortly after it went public and proved to be a business whose products had a growing fan following.

In 1999, three years after going public, Harsh received a call from Keki Dadiseth, chairman and managing director, HLL, many times the size of Marico. Lever already had a reasonable presence in the coconut oil market, having acquired Cococare and Nihar from TOMCO, and the multinational was covetously eyeing Parachute. Dadiseth informed Mariwala that Lever proposed to buy Parachute and assured Mariwala, 'I will give you enough resources to take care of yourself and all future generations.' He went on to inform unambiguously that 'If I did not sell, then I would be the loser, as HLL would make sure that there would be nothing left of Parachute in the market.'[14] How did the founder respond?

Right there over the phone, Mariwala's response was 'Mr Dadiseth, you may think I am a nut, but you will find

---

[14]Sonu Bhasin, *The Inheritors: Stories of Entrepreneurship and Success,* Portfolio, Chapter 2, 2017

that I am a tough nut to crack. Thanks, but no thanks!'[15] Harsh took this stand despite the 'sage' counsel of bankers to strike a good deal. His response was illustrative of his commitment to the future of his company built with 'toil, sweat and tears.' Harsh was deeply influenced by Professor Ram Charan, the corporate expert who advised Harsh for Marico. Regarding Parachute, Professor Charan had said, 'Come what may, you need to protect your resource-generating engine.' The inference was clear—if Harsh was committed to Marico's future, sale of Parachute would not be negotiable. The situation reflected the undaunted spirit and determination of the Indian entrepreneur pitched against the might of the MNC enjoying a market capitalization about 50 times greater.

The marketing giant unleashed an advertising and discounting war against Parachute and the first round of the battle impacted Marico severely in the stock market. HLL won some market share for its competing coconut oil brand Nihar, pitted against Parachute. Marico was undeterred and fought back by emphasizing the superior product quality of Parachute with the '*Shuddhata ka Seal*' (The seal of purity) campaign and by an accelerated expansion of distribution in the rural areas. Marico raised the morale of its extended field force and distributors with a stirring, spirit-lifting battle response: '*Parachute ki kasam.*' (Parachute's promise). The brand stoically held onto its market share, although margins were impacted. Marico's employees and business partners rallied together in this battle for survival with self-respect. This was not the walkover that Goliath had anticipated. Not making

---

[15]Sonu Bhasin, *The Inheritors: Stories of Entrepreneurship and Success*, Portfolio, Chapter 2, 2017

a show of bravado by going to court, seeking an intervention from 'influentials', or self-destructing in retaliation, this David responded with a typical, daring 'trademark innovation' defence! HLL carried on the expense-backed attack and did manage to notch a double-digit share that was largely at the expense of other brands. However, this battle ended in an anti-climax.

HLL soon received directions from its London headquarters to call off the confrontation as Unilever had decided that coconut oil was not of global interest for the multinational! The real climax of the story is as climactic as the commencement.

Poetic Justice: Six years later, when HLL put up its Nihar coconut oil brand for sale, Mariwala took the call that coconut oil was very much in Marico's interest. He acquired the brand from the multinational! Once again, Harsh displayed uncommon thinking, showing unflinching conviction in the importance of coconut oil for Marico, despite the concerns expressed by stock market analysts.

Marico's innovation, stakeholder orientation and entrepreneurial culture are the defining elements of the Marico story. Great companies believe that corporations have a purpose at the core beyond satisfying stakeholders' needs. These are to improve the lives of users, ensure financial viability and provide returns to investors—a theme that reverberates with Marico, which has happily begun to gain acceptance with leaders of corporate India and fellow business academics too.

Over the years, Marico has added and shed products in its portfolio basket in India and abroad in keeping with the company's criteria of featuring within the top two or three players holding market share for that category. So while Parachute and Saffola remain Marico's premium brands, it expanded into new products and brand extensions within the personal and home care categories, as we shall see in the next chapter, which also explores how this consumer products company manages its multi-brand portfolio.

Chapter 5

Innovative Brand Architect

Harsh's field visits early in his career were voyages of discovery for the young scion. His passion was to scale up Marico's business by building brands and extending reach to win and retain customers. Harsh understood that as growth was deeply linked with regular introduction of new products and brand extensions, the funding for product innovation was a prerequisite. Harsh states, 'We learnt from Prof. Ram Charan that you should preserve 15 per cent of company profits towards strategic funding by design and accept that's the hit you're prepared to take.' This hit was the 'affordable loss' for the company in its pursuit of innovation.

Compare this guideline of funding for innovation with the no-holds-barred venture capital approach of lavishing start-ups with funds for chasing 'take-off' volume growth, driven by the shared obsession to achieve 'unicorn' valuation. These companies may never achieve profits, without which disruption—both financial and social—is inevitable. After all, the only thing that matters to all stakeholders is profits and eventually the unicorn companies would need to have the plug pulled when the mirage is realized, leaving the venture and the founder high and dry![16] The situation has its parallel in India and it is the antithesis of the Marico way of growth through value innovation.

Harsh understood that valuation distracts from building brand value. So, he focused on first building value for Marico's key brands—Parachute and Saffola. Harsh had his ear to the ground and listened to the people who mattered—from distributors to customers—to deliver benefits as desired by the end customer. He was conscious that coconut oil was not within the radar of MNCs abroad or in India, which meant brand-related expenses would be affordable and not prohibitively expensive. Parachute was, thus, marketed to retailers and directed to customers through a multimedia promotion campaign with the tagline, 'Parachute is a promise'. Marico was a pioneer among Indian FMCG companies in deriving competitive advantage through design and execution of a brand vision that Indians of the post–independence era bought into. As a desirable brand, Parachute was on the highway to market leadership at higher profit, which was a first for a coconut oil on a national scale.

The core of Marico's uncommon strategy has been to create a growing market for consumer brands in categories where the competition is unbranded or is offering local brands and where MNCs are unlikely to enter, like in the categories of coconut oil, safflower oil or even anti-lice treatment. This approach also guided its choice of emerging global markets

---

[16]Sandipan Deb, 'The disappearance of management mantras', Livemint, 11 December 2019. Available at: https://www.livemint.com/news/india/thedisappearance-of-management-mantras-11575986622513.html

like Bangladesh and even influenced its acquisition strategy.

Harsh was completely committed to profitable growth unlike the archetypal venture capital funded, valuation-obsessed entrepreneurs of the day. He was clear that in terms of direction, Marico's growth path should be focused on beauty and wellness, product categories ready for growth in India and in the emerging markets of the world. Marico's domain focus remain Beauty and Wellness with a broadening of the portfolios through brand extensions or acquisitions enveloping the sub-domains of hair care, healthcare, skincare and male grooming in beauty, and healthy foods in the wellness category.

NEW BRANDS AND EXTENSIONS

Harsh believed that while Parachute and Saffola would continue to grow profitably, the way forward for Marico was to extend the brand portfolio. From the mid-1990s, Marico launched product extensions for these brands backed up by four manufacturing facilities in Maharashtra and Kerala and dedicated third-party manufacturing sources for hair care and fabric care. Harsh realized that managing the portfolio is a crucial activity for a consumer products company and contract manufacturing under strict quality control allows entrepreneurial attention to be directed to the core task of generating customer traction. Depending on the volume outsourced for manufacture and the period, reputed, profitable companies marketing leading brands through a well-developed distribution network could negotiate win-win terms. They could insist on exclusivity and institute detailed quality and output norms. As Unilever co-chairman Niall FitzGerald said, 'We're not a manufacturing company anymore. We're a brand marketing group that happens to make some of its products.'

A steady stream of new products, mostly as brand extensions, were launched, serving niche markets. After all, as marketing guru David Aacker prescribes, a strong brand association provides a point of differentiation and advantage for the extension, which proved favourable for Parachute Advansed coconut oil, although not for Parachute Amla oil, Saffola packaged pulses, Saffola Oats and even Saffola Zest, a health snack launched after a market research study! Marico realized that it had focused on health and neglected taste, which did not work for Indian consumers. This is something that a customer insight study could possibly have revealed better than a market research study. The lesson learnt was not to disrupt the food market at the cost of taste. This truth was borne out by the success of Saffola Masala Oats, a blue ocean category not inhabited by the giants, Kellog's and Quaker. For Harsh, it's the little nuggets of consumer insights that make a company large. Marico is a prime example of that. Sounds like uncommon sense, yet, only a learning mindset can distil a business opportunity from a welter of information.

Harsh also believed that fast-track growth could only come from innovation, whereby Marico's modern, well-equipped laboratory in Mumbai developed a spiel of new products ranging from non-sticky hair oil, Hair & Care, targeted at millennials to Revive fabric starch, which was an instant success.

TAKEOVER BRANDS

All around Marico, FMCG start-ups founded by new-generation entrepreneurs—unburdened by complacency and brought about by success—were blooming. These ventures had the chutzpah to discern and ride the wave of new technology or business model innovation—namely cost-effective marketing through e-commerce marketplaces side-stepping the conventional distribution channel. Cheaper, private labels fuelled by retail discounters, online and offline, were beginning to occupy niches. The new entrants are not always priced lower in their product offerings though. Nouveau brands have surfaced in India using high-quality ingredients and taking premium positioning. It began with food and beverage brand Paperboat in year 2012, which was the forerunner of a stream of upmarket consumer product start-ups. Brands like Fit and Glow in beauty and MCaffeine in the personal care category, including shower gels and face wash, were the combined efforts of R&D, communicating the brand value proposition to the millennial customer and getting the eye and the purse of the investor to fund the ramp up. The larger mainstream players were beginning to notice the impact of some of these quick-footed start-ups.

Marico responded to this burgeoning presence through acquisition of new-age 'growing up' brands that have passed the customer acceptance stage just as the Unilevers, the Reckitt Benckisers, the Danones and their MNC ilk are doing. Marico has pursued the acquisition route, more so as an emerging market MNC.

Marico scanned the consumer goods market for potential

acquisitions in the beauty and wellness category to sustain its growth momentum. Mediker, an anti-lice treatment shampoo from the P&G India stable, was Marico's first acquisition in 2007, as P&G realized that treatment for anti-lice was not a perceived need for upper-income families. The product found favour among the rural populace. P&G had launched Mediker in a shampoo format, an inhibiting factor for rural households. The product received moderate effort from the sales force and enjoyed only moderate success. Marico's 'homework' or market research revealed the target customer segment's uneasiness with shampooing. With this information and its knowledge of hair oil, Marico's R&D transferred the anti-lice properties to an oil base. Thus transformed, Mediker was a hit!

Marico also went on to acquire men's grooming brand, Beardo, from an Ahmedabad-based start-up Zed Lifestyle, which had made inroads in this category. This marked Marico's entry into male grooming products, a new segment under the beauty and wellness category.

Having developed the taste for acquisitions, Marico went on a shopping spree. In 2010, Marico acquired the hair styling brand 'Code 10' from Colgate-Palmolive and bought out the aesthetics business of Singapore-based Derma Rx Asia Pacific in the skincare range. In 2011, Marico acquired an 85 per cent stake in Vietnamese firm International Consumer Products, which has a presence in the personal care, cosmetics, sauces and condiments categories.

Harsh could see that Indians were moving away from a savings-centric orientation to being consumption centric. Sensing the shift in consumer behaviour, Marico acquired Paras Pharma's personal care portfolio from Reckitt and

Benkiser for ₹740 crore in 2012, which included brands like Set Wet hair gel for men, Zatak Deo, and Livon, a hair serum, both viable start-up acquisitions, providing Marico a head start in developing related brands for the new generation. Marico has made 12 acquisitions in 12 years.

Marico worked to integrate these brands into its portfolio of existing brands. Brand building is not synonymous with just acquiring a brand and building the image of the brand. It is the outcome of managing all aspects of contact that the customer would have with the brand, such as packaging, pricing, perception and distribution over and above differentiated product quality. For instance, Marico succeeded in elevating its coconut oil from the category of a home commodity with a name, to a sought-after national brand. If over time the brand has retained its value with customers, it is due to sustained efforts to be relevant with changing customer behaviour.

As a company with a portfolio of successful brands, Marico had to face its own share of challenges when competitors rapidly copied new brand features, effectively destroying the product differentiation and the cause for brand premium. In such a situation, how does a company sustain the differentiation. For example, marketing coffee powder as packaged instant coffee brand is a solution as it reduces customer time for preparing coffee. Lakmé tried to extend its product range from beauty care products to branded beauty salons to counter the lure of foreign brands. This strategy is beneficial for the brand if it retains or enhances loyalty and enables premium pricing. Firmly entrenched in the FMCG sector, Marico too continued to explore the breadth of innovation in beauty products. Its cosmetics story will be incomplete without inclusion of its foray into service with Kaya Skincare Clinics.

KAYA: DEEP SKIN SERVICE

There is a story about Marico's foray into Kaya. The year was 2002 and Marico was a cash-rich, debt-free FMCG company known for innovation. After a visit to London, Harsh was drawn to the idea of starting a chain of skincare clinics. He figured that 'hiring a dermatologist would be much cheaper in India', quite oblivious of the unconventionality of consumer product companies venturing into retail clinics.

On the basis of customer insights and market research, Marico developed a new brand designed to be scalable. In partnership with a friend of Harsh, whose stake was subsequently bought out, Marico spread its wings in 2002 to float Kaya Skin Care Solutions, provider of skincare and allied beauty solutions, creating a unique niche brand that combine products and services for skincare. For instance, its skincare services including acne, pigmentation and anti-aging, recommends use of in-house developed products. The business model for Kaya Clinic is marrying skincare as a service with skincare products developed by Marico R&D. The challenge in this business model is in lowering overheads of the clinic and pricing the service at a premium, yet drawing a clientele to the clinic to derive profits at the unit level.

When queried why Marico, a reputed FMCG player, chose to break tradition by diverting to start a solutions business, Harsh said,

In retrospect, Marico is the only example I know of a product player that has ventured into what we call solutions. We will be more and more involved with going into solutions. If you have a problem with your skin, say pimples, you will just go and buy a cream. As opposed to this, when you go to Kaya you will get customized treatment by a specialist doctor, a dermatologist, and then you may avail of services, products and a special recommended diet. The whole 360-degree customized approach to skincare, haircare or wellness is far more effective than just using a product. Another reason was that we wanted to enter the skincare space and felt that going only through the product route would make it difficult for us to become market leaders in this highly competitive market. So we decided to take on a service route and create a brand. Of course, we also have products under Kaya.[17]

Harsh's clarity on winning market leadership with a differentiated branded service is quite evident even though making the venture consistently in the black has taken much effort.

In actioning the Kaya initiative, Marico had to step out of the conventional branding mode for FMCG and come to grips with reality. To quote Mariwala, 'In FMCG business we manufacture and distribute our brands to retailers and create demand through advertising. We don't interact with

---

[17]Management During Changing Times: The Case of Marico Industries with Harsh Mariwala, Indian Institute of Management, Bangalore, 2014. Available at: https://tejas.iimb.ac.in/interviews/08.php

customers. In a service business, however, we are dealing with individual customers and individual feedback. We had to change our way of advertising, as our service brand didn't have a budget as large as our FMCG brands. Further, if you put an FMCG person in charge, he will handle it with an FMCG mindset, which is not the way to handle a service brand. We identified Marico people having a flexible mindset required for the service industry and gave them the required freedom. They reported to me directly in Kaya's formative years.'[18]

It took the business a decade to make profits when the number of retail units totalled 85. The venture was then hived off as a listed subsidiary. Two new formats were launched— Kaya skin bars, which were smaller format stores to sell Kaya products and an e-commerce site called shop.kayaclinic.com. The focus on product sales led to higher footfalls and sales through a shift in positioning from 'cure' to 'prevention and cure'. As Harsh said, 'This shift along with the acquisition of the Derma Rx premium range of skincare products has been a key factor for the turnaround in Kaya's business.'[19] By year 2018, Kaya operated in 105 centres in India and 19 in the Middle East.

What is Harsh's rationale for sticking with the business despite the hiccups? He responds, 'We look at businesses from a long-term perspective, through the lens of sustainable growth with a clear visibility of profitability.'

Reflecting on Marico's Kaya adventure, Harsh muses,

---

[18]'Interview with Harsh Mariwala by Rajesh Srivastava', *IIM Indore*, 1(3), Oct–Dec 2009.
[19]'Interview with Harsh Mariwala by Rajesh Srivastava', *IIM Indore*, 1(3), Oct–Dec 2009.

'The skincare solution was a different business for us at the intersection of retail, hospitality and medical businesses and entering it was certainly not a mistake. We did go through a learning curve and the insight was that we ramped up too fast.' He goes on to acknowledge the challenges primarily from smaller players with virtually no overhead costs.

In year 2013, Kaya demerged from Marico. Explaining the rationale for separating Kaya from Marico, Harsh commented, 'The demerger of Kaya was meant to facilitate the consolidation of Marico's business in India and overseas.'[20] It is a fact that the success factors for building a service business like Kaya are different from those relevant to succeed in growing an FMCG business. To exploit the potentially large opportunity, Kaya had to constantly absorb investments that would have inevitably impacted the financial position of the listed parent company. Investors were not unanimous on how much and for how long Marico would have to bear the financial load. The only way out was separation of the two different businesses.

Kaya, now positioned as a grooming chain, has recently entered into a licencing arrangement with Marico for creating and selling brand Kaya Youth, a new range of skincare products. This is a win-win relationship for both. Says Saugata, 'While Kaya has high brand salience, distribution is limited to mostly its own clinics. Marico's new range will be at a mass-premium level to make it more accessible and also have a

---

[20]'Leadership Unplugged, How Harsh Mariwala Led Several Transformations at Marico.' Available at: http://www.leadershipunplugged.in/how-harsh-mariwala-led-several-transformations-at-marico/

wider distribution.' For Marico, it serves the twin objectives of reducing dependence on Parachute and Saffola brands and shifting focus to the premium segment of its portfolio.

MANAGING BRAND PORTFOLIO

As we can see from Harsh's struggles and innovations with Parachute, merely imposing a name on a product does not make it a brand. Brands need to highlight the differentiation from a commodity product. It is the association of the features and attributes of the product to functional and emotional benefits for a particular customer segment that transforms it into a brand. Branding is a crucial activity for a consumer product company, which needs to be sustained with tenacity and innovation.

Marico did this while constantly adding and subtracting brands from its product portfolio in India and overseas, guided by the primary criteria—its position as a market leader. Is there no limit to expanding the range of a brand portfolio? How many brands can a portfolio sustain?

Professor Nirmalya Kumar, marketing faculty at Singapore Management University, developed a set of criteria to determine brand success and the number of brands a portfolio can sustain. Marico's portfolio of brands may be validated against these touchstones, namely, brand position in the market, advertising expenditure vis-à-vis competitors, competition between brands and overlaps in terms of the brand's target segment, product lines, price bands and distribution channels. Marico's brand portfolio rates positively on each of these criteria as its strategy is to play in spaces where its brands qualify the Right to Win criteria. Consequently, more than 90 per cent of Marico brands rank among the top three players in the category.

Marico relies on the consumer insighting process for determining the value proposition of every brand and brand extension. It allocates a marketing budget for each brand and then supports its new brands till they acquire critical mass by volume and margins before the budget is exhausted. Marico also has an annual budget for strategic innovation on the basis of which funds and R&D manpower are allocated. Decisions on resource allocation are based on the priorities set in the Strategic Business Plan annually and there are no 'escape buttons' for taking time over decision-making. Further, the organizational culture of transparency and openness facilitates learning through cooperation and recognition for merit. Managers are regularly shifted across departments to develop a holistic view of their work. Marico has always endeavoured to not only advertise the brand, but live it, as Nirmalya advises. To this may be added, in thought, word and deed and importantly, over time, which is actually the acid test for a brand retaining its position in the higher reaches of the brand pyramid.

Mariwala's unswerving commitment to value-based growth with profit through trust and empowerment of the company's 'members' and by branding innovative Right to Win products helped Marico emerge as a leading Indian FMCG with an extensive portfolio of products. With a presence in India and emerging markets across Asia and Africa, Marico is a household name that touches the lives of one out of every three Indians today.[21] Its journey is a saga of building sustainable business institutions, as we shall see in the next chapter.

---

[21]*Marico Annual Report,* 2018–19.

Chapter 6

Institutional Transformation

Marico, seeded in BOIL, and a Gen-Liberalization company, has taken a sustained growth path in the last 30 years doing business in a dynamic FMCG sector marked by changing consumer preferences, in the process laying claim to becoming a business institution. As a business, Marico has added value to the lives of its customers, employees, associates, investors, the state and society while remaining true to its purpose and values. Marico's claim to becoming an institution is in the foundation laid to perpetuate this model, going forward. How has Mariwala shaped Marico as an institution?

For a venture to grow sustainably, both entrepreneurship and bureaucracy are needed. It is not a trade-off of one for the other. Bureaucratic work conditions destroy initiative: it is the common belief that working in bureaucratic organizations suppresses entrepreneurship. Yet, bureaucracy constitutes the most efficient and rational way to organize human activity in terms of systematic processes and hierarchies to facilitate continuous growth. Harsh shaped Marico to achieve the desired balance between the two forces for generating accelerated growth with profit. In his mind they were not forces in opposition, they were enablers to be harnessed.

ENTREPRENEURIAL BUREAUCRACY

Business, whether yesterday, today or tomorrow, always commences as a start-up by the entrepreneur, then scales up by hiring employees, creating value and generating revenues. Hiring staff leads to job descriptions, supervisory and subordinate roles, and accounting for incomes and expenses, resulting in processes and systems that constitute bureaucracy. In time, entrepreneurship is usually taken over by bureaucracy. This is how management rationalizes the hold of bureaucracy in an organization.

An analogy can be drawn with Scott Fitzerland's *The Curious Case of Benjamin Button,* a popular story set in the 1860s. In the story, the protagonist, Benjamin Button, is a man who reverse ages. Born as a frail wispy-haired old man, Benjamin's body grows bigger and more manlike every year while his face grows younger and more juvenile. As Benjamin ages backward and becomes younger, he has a wealth of relevant knowledge and ideas to share with the modernizing world, having already experienced life as an older citizen. Can we extrapolate the situation in this story to the life cycle of a venture and make some conjectures?

The pendulum of any institution swings from one end—the experimental ways of starting up, the child-like curiosity and learning —to the other end, the reality of age bringing with it a fixed mindset and ways of working. Using the metaphor of the Benjamin Button story, it can be said that every entrepreneur and CEO would like to run his or her business in 'entrepreneurship bureaucracy' mode, enjoying the best of both states! Succeeding in managing a profitably growing business requires a spirit to dare without being shackled with the fear of failure, the learnability and flexibility of a start-up entrepreneur supported by the systems and processes, the job descriptions and the supervisory function—the role of bureaucracy—for building sustainably on success. As an organization grows, its complexity ensures that a certain measure of 'professional' bureaucracy is inevitable. Striking a balance between being process driven and individual driven without getting stuck in between is the challenge that the organization has to come to terms with. This is easier said than done.

Most governmental organizations, for instance, may have been set up as oxygen-producing trees, to assist growth. However, collectively the trees morphed as a dense forest difficult to navigate. So too with ventures that adopt processes and systems to enable smooth decision-making only to eventually get trapped in the same rules and regulations alias, conventional bureaucracy. The process of following procedures while chasing accelerated growth gets to be at cross purposes with a culture that encourages entrepreneurial spirit, flexibility and adaptability. Developing a simple, helpful bureaucracy that facilitates getting new things done well and in time, with the hindsight of experience, is a sign of entrepreneurial bureaucracy. Marico has been able to achieve this feat. For instance, the majority of Marico's Board consists of members with diverse and truly independent CEO profiles from the

FMCG and consumer services sectors and with proven credentials in driving sustainable results while practising corporate governance. Their role is to enable Marico's TMT to achieve business goals in the spirit of the purpose, values and business direction adopted by the organization.

Mariwala has painstakingly shaped Marico's organizational culture to be conducive to entrepreneurial behaviour backed by a supportive bureaucracy. When we asked Mariwala how he was able to fine-tune the organization in this manner, aligning the best aspects of both, he shed light on the building blocks.

> What I look for in a Mariconian is quality talent with self-motivation to improve, overcome barriers and bounce from setbacks. For the organization, it is critical to create the right culture to bring out the best in people. A culture that is suited for the business of consumer products. For organizational culture building, we needed to focus on what kind of values are relevant to succeed in our business and accordingly design the culture. For it to succeed, I think a lot depends on how top management behaves, what kind of signals they give and how they reinforce values. The key is quality talent that is self-motivated and provided with an opportunity to continuously improve, backed up by a supportive culture. In our case it is an open culture, a trust-based culture, an empowering culture, merit-based culture, experimental- and innovation-driven culture, all the factors relevant to our business.

Harsh's clarity on 'relevance to our business' is in terms of Marico shaping up as an emerging market Indian FMCG corporation on level terms with the entrenched global FMCG MNCs in the country.

***Open Door Policy*:** Marico as an institution has 'walked the talk' in all these aspects since Harsh founded the company, back in the 1990s. In the start-up phase, Harsh set the stage for an entrepreneurial culture by having an open office backed up by the norm of Mariconians addressing each other by their first names, by no means company practice then or even now. The managing director himself was no exception to this office norm of first name calling although it must have taken some guts for a fresh recruit to hail Mariwala, walking around the office, by his first name, to catch his attention! Eventually, they got used to it, helped no doubt, by Harsh's open door policy. Did team work inducing informality in organizational behaviour oust traditional bureaucracy?

Harsh figuratively followed up on his open door policy by reinforcing the belief that it was okay to disagree professionally for the benefit of the business. Harsh not only takes independence in contributing to discussions in his stride, he welcomes being critiqued irrespective of seniority. He feels criticizers are a dime a dozen offering no value addition unlike someone providing an informed, balanced critique on his approach or on Marico.

Job Rotation: Marico staff can, in practice, interact with anyone at all levels across functions without need for prior sanction from the boss. Employees are encouraged to share information with different divisions of the company. A simple transparent process for becoming efficient and effective at the job. To foster better appreciation of the contribution of every function, the company adopted the practice of job rotation. This practice was applied to the top management, too, through the growth stage, an affirmation that no silos existing anywhere. Job rotation was not a mere HR experiment, it was also to spark innovation, a fresh approach to the job at hand and to develop a holistic view for different roles. At the TMT level, Jeswant Nair, vice president HR, took over as head of sales, and Rakesh Pandey, general manager operations, became chief HR officer. Middle and junior managers and staff continue to practice job rotation.

Failure is Learning: What has brought success to Marico as a leading Indian FMCG company is innovation. Since its birth, Marico has been an innovator in products, processes and practices. Innovation requires trying out something not done earlier, that need not always succeed. Bureaucracy generally inhibits risk taking in employees, instilling the fear of failure and blame apportioning in case the experiment does not produce expected results. To offset this innovation spoiler, Mariwala's approach has been 'you win or you learn.' In other words, it is okay to fail as long as you learn from the experiment and the monetary cost is within affordable limits. Professor R.A. Mashelkar, Chairman of the Marico Innovation Foundation, puts this in his own creative way as FAIL stands for 'First Attempt In Learning.' Eliminating the fear of failure is a huge spur to innovate.

EMPOWERMENT WITH TRUST

Striking the right balance in a growing business like Marico between encouraging entrepreneurship and alignment with business direction involved matching job descriptions with appropriate authority and responsibility. Accountability with empowerment as required for doing the job exceptionally well is beneficial both for the company and employees. Marico believes that empowerment combined with the 'you win or you learn' approach makes the company an attractive place to work for the best of talent. After all, the acid test of an entrepreneurial bureaucracy is the experience of employee empowerment by employees in the organization.

Mariwala's efforts since Marico's inception have been to create the cultural environment for a highly productive organization. Accordingly, its organizational design is based on two core beliefs, trust and empowerment—the underlying principles on which roles are designed at Marico. Unlike most MNCs based in India, Marico's emphasis on employee empowerment is aided by its flat organization structure with just five levels between the MD and the office staffer or factory worker at the lowest rung of the hierarchy. This has motivated Mariconians to deliver superior performance.

Another instance of Marico enshrining trust with employees is in empowering them with keeping their own attendance and leave records! At Marico, HR neither monitors employees' attendance nor maintains leave records and reimbursements for expenses incurred at work are self-administered. Through empowerment, Marico did away with routine bureaucracy.

It is rightly said that trust begets trusts. Particularly when the culture is 'right'. Employees bear the responsibility to honour the trust imposed on them, which is how Marico empowers its employees. While not expecting such empowerment to be misused, the consequence of misuse is a prompt exit for the employee. True employee empowerment leads to employee engagement, impacting employee, and thereby, organization performance.

So how can leaders empower their employees? Organizations like Google, Disney and Four Seasons are household names and well-known for going above and beyond to empower their employees. As Murielle Tiambo, Strategy Consultant, PwC notes, 'When leaders understand that employee empowerment is paramount to achieving organizational goals, they realize that people are their most strategic assets; all other organizational elements—technology, products, processes—result from the actions of employees.[22]

Truly, it is only when employees feel empowered and aligned with organizational values, do they go the extra mile to contribute to the company's purpose and create value to customers.

Empowerment also calls for employee autonomy to make decisions and be accountable for results. For example in the asset management firm, Tiambo, the leadership team had taken deliberate and consistent actions to empower its

[22]Murielle Tiambo, Leaders Can Cultivate True Employee Empowerment, *Forbes*, 29 February 2019, https://www.forbes.com/sites/strategyand/2019/02/19/leaders-can-cultivate-true-employee-empowerment/#7fd9c2ab3ab1

people by giving them enough opportunities to take on new challenges and grow their skills sets. However, its employees did not feel empowered, stating that their leaders would give them responsibilities but fail to let go of authority. For instance, an experienced staff member working on a deal would be stopped from closing it because the deal was deemed too risky or not appropriate higher up in the hierarchy. Sometimes it would take two months for a team to convince senior executives to close a deal, while competitors might take two weeks.

The lack of agility had led many team members to become hesitant about their ability to assure investment partners that they could take the deal over the finish line, leading them to miss out on opportunities to bring in new business. Many studies have proved a high correlation between creativity and autonomy. Empowerment or freedom is understood as reposing trust in employees to think and act autonomously in sync with the organization. However, leaders, concerns about empowering employees relate to the possibility of indiscipline at work. What seems self-evident can thus be challenging to practise. Marico seems to have found the method for empowering employees for better performance. Credit goes to Harsh for his unwavering commitment to this practice that has now been institutionalized through a well-aligned HR function.

Freedom within a Framework: Is there a way to overcome the apprehension of senior management that 'loss of control' through empowerment would impact organization discipline? There is.

Research work conducted by Professor Ranjay Gulati, Faculty at Harvard Business School, showed that there was a pattern in the manner organizations across a wide range of industries had succeeded in instituting effective empowerment. They had a set of guidelines, which were truly guidelines and not controls in any way, that were acceptable and could be internalized. Leaders of the companies studied by Gulati had enabled employee freedom under a framework that embedded the organization's purpose, priorities and principles as a set of guidelines. 'Freedom within a framework' is how such leaders described their winning 'formula'. Trusting employees to work without controls is not in the interest of the company. A blend of freedom and aligned responsibility is the solution.

Marico fares well on Gulati's guidelines, which promise freedom within a framework, when well designed and implemented, by giving people a clear, positive, galvanizing sense of where the organization is trying to go.[23] Employees or members of the Marico family are indoctrinated without exception with the company's purpose during their induction programme. The alignment with the purpose is reinforced annually, commencing with an address by Harsh and followed by events like audio-visuals of 'being more, everyday.'

The values inculcated into Mariconians, like commitment to merit on the job, and the belief 'you win or you learn', underling innovation conforms to Gulati's guidelines. Also, Marico's commitment for developing Right to Win products has served to empower its employees to be genuinely innovative. The defining characteristic of a Right to Win

[23]Ranjay Gulati, 'Managing Organisations, Structure That's Not Stifling', *Harvard Business Review*, May–June 2018.

product is a differentiated package of benefits to the target customer segment. For example, the purity, transparency and aroma of Parachute coconut oil from Marico delivered tangible features plus the intangible value of brand Marico in one Right to Win package.

At the core, empowerment as configured in the mind of the top management gets translated across the organization. The key question is does the CEO walk the talk in thought, word and deed? It is a touchy subject, but Harsh clarifies that the starting point for empowerment is at the top. As the founder of Marico, he feels that the growth of the company is a shared responsibility. 'If founders believe that they alone are responsible for the growth of the company, then success can go to their head. They begin thinking they are the cat's whiskers because they think they know everything. Such whiskered autocrats either do not recruit good talent or if they do, they will not delegate. They also tend to maintain tight control that totally demotivates organizational talent,' Harsh is convinced. 'Only the top management can empower employees. That is all,' he adds.

Demonstrating the flow of empowerment from the top, Harsh snapped the 'family line' of authority in Marico in 2014, by handing over the responsibility of this institution to Saugata Gupta, Marico's Chief Operating Officer (COO), who is not a family member, thus rendering Marico for the record as a family-owned business, but no longer a family, managed business.

Failure is Acceptable: Under Mariwala's guidance, Marico implemented employee empowerment. When we asked him how empowerment had become a part of company culture, he said, 'People should experiment without being afraid to fail. If you are afraid, then you stop taking risk and that cannot augur well for our commitment to continuous innovation. It is with experiment that Marico has evolved, there is nothing like either you win or you fail. You learn and cannot lose.' A clear message down the line empowered Marico employees to fail within set affordable loss limits.

Hands Off, Mind On: Harsh has gone through the process of shedding authority—from being hands on, to getting things done through leading a talented TMT, to influencing Mariconians. 'My role has changed now. Earlier Marico was a promoter-driven company. Now I see my role as a strategic investor. I still manage the Board, but on a day-to-day basis nothing comes to me. Even if I am away for a month, I will still not get a single phone call,' Harsh elaborates.

So, while many company leaders espouse employee empowerment, few walk the talk to rise to the challenge of giving up power for the benefit of the company. The experience at Marico is that empowerment at all levels is genuinely beneficial to the institution. Mariwala is now 'hands off, mind on' with Marico.

SUCCESSION PLANNING

A leader cannot go on forever and succession planning and leadership development are vital elements in an organization's transformation to an institution.

Saugata who replaced Harsh, joined Marico in 2004 as

Head of Marketing. He was an active participant in the culture, building processes at Marico. Impressed with his performance and ability to grasp the critical success factors of the business, he was promoted to COO.

In keeping with the company's culture of transparency, sometime in 2014, Saugata expressed to Harsh that he felt he could do more. Harsh, conscious that he had built Marico as a 'family owned, professionally managed' company emphasizing merit with values, recommended to the Board that Saugata should succeed him as he felt that Saugata was best qualified for the job.

Between Mariwala and the Board, a process was designed to effect a smooth transition. As desired by the Board, both Harsh as non-executive Chairman of the Board and Saugata as incumbent CEO and Managing Director, wrote their detailed responsibilities and role descriptions to guide them in their working and discovered that these were much in alignment.

Six years hence, Harsh's role is to work with the Board and Saugata takes up the day-to-day operations of the company. The company has marched ahead in this time, which is testimony to the merit-based company culture that ensures absence of groupism at the Board and the TMT.

Externally, it was surprising that a family member did not succeed Mariwala, a practice prevalent among family-owned enterprises. In sharp contrast, Mariwala practised what he preached about merit for the job as the selection criterion for all designations and chose as his successor someone who, as Mariwala stated, 'is better than me for this job now.'

Considering the tremors caused by the Securities and Exchange Board of India's ruling to separate the functions of chairman and Managing Director and to have one of them as a non-family member, we were curious about Mariwala's choice of successor. When questioned, he said, 'Indian society is hierarchical and expects that the son will be the successor. But to me, the issue was, what is good for the organization has to come first.'

The ability to look ahead and develop a succession plan is a key behavioural trait of business founders that marks their transformation from a leader to a shaper who influences without authority; it is critical for a company to evolve as a business institution. Replacing himself as Managing Director and CEO with a company professional on merit, while yet eliciting a market response of 'Why' and not 'Why Not', was Mariwala's tipping contribution to shaping Marico as a business institution.

Mariwala's son Rishab is now a Marico Board member. He had worked in Marico for some years in a middle management marketing role. As Harsh implies, 'After me, he will be a non-executive chairman without being Managing Director.' In this manner, the issue of succession was institutionalized at Marico during the tenure of the founder. This is especially relevant considering that succession within the family in Indian family businesses is taken for granted. This was revealed in a study by the Indian School of Business (ISB), the Thomas Schmidheiny Centre for Family Enterprise, which surveyed 53 family businesses in India.[24] In fact, only few

[24]*The Economic Times,* 'Most Family Businesses in India Have No Planned Succession: Survey, 6 November 2019. Available at: https://economictimes.indiatimes.com/news/company/corporate-trends/most-family-businesses-in-indiahave-no-planned-succession-survey/

family businesses, unable to face the critical challenges of governance and succession planning, can survive beyond the third generation.

As we can see, Mariwala evolved Marico into a business institution in three distinct ways: achieving entrepreneurial bureaucracy for governance, employee empowerment and succession planning. With a clear governance structure and cohesion within the Board, a family business need not cease to exist without a family member as head of the organization despite majority ownership by the family.

Indian family businesses account for 64 per cent of all companies and contribute 25 per cent to the national economy. Governance and family cohesion are the primary challenges for survival of family businesses. How to meet these challenges and survive?

Says Frank Stangenberg-Haverkamp, chairman of E. Merck KG, a German healthcare and life sciences MNC, which is a successful family business with a 350-year legacy spanning 13 generations. 'For business families to last beyond the third generation, the most important thing to do is to draw up a family contract early, very early—in the second generation itself when there are less people involved. The family contract or any legally binding written document should lay down all the rules and regulations for eventualities that a good family lawyer would know, and come up with a good draft, one that will make it difficult for a family member to opt out of that contract. You must clearly define a family member and ensure that all participate.'[25]

articleshow/71940464.cms?from=mdr
[25]Business Today, 'A Family Member Is Only a Trustee', 16 June 2019.

Haverkamp is an eleventh-generation leader and knows what he is talking about. The E. Merck family business is a much-quoted example of family leadership continuity coupled with long-term business sustainability. Haverkamp believes that family members are only the trustees and have a duty to pass on the share of the company to their children and grandchildren because many people who work for the company and their families are dependent on it.

Undeniably, business performance has an impact beyond the family. It therefore makes sense that business families operate under guidelines governing decision-making on key issues like succession and leadership, pre-empting conflict, distribution of profit and other contentious issues that can seriously impact business. The quality of the decisions impacts not only their wealth, it also affects the employees and the ecosystem in which the business operates.

What is needed for continuity is for business families to create an operating model that enables them to manage effectively, treat family members fairly and pre-empt conflict to overcome the challenges of governance and cohesion. Following an exhaustive study of multi-generation family business globally, consulting firm BCG proposed a four-step format that serves as an operating model for the longevity of a family business. It covers the following: (*i*) clarity and agreement on the family's overarching goal and business priority that best suits its values, to determine the business strategy and operating principles; (*ii*) Early anticipation and identification of potential hotspots and flashpoints

Available at https://www.businesstoday.in/magazine/the-hub/a-family-member-is-only-a-trustee/story/350804.html that could cause conflict and derail harmony and business success; (*iii*) review of the family business structure—for example, ownership—necessitated by a number of factors like changes in family members' involvement, in the nature of the group holding, going public, or even by changes in the industry, regulations and in legal aspects; and (*iv*) decision on governing structure through an appropriate Shareholders' Agreement including a family code of conduct. In essence these are the beliefs that drive Mariwala's vision for Marico.

Clearly, there is no shortcut to building a lasting business with a strong foundation. As Harsh notes, 'Family accountability is the biggest barometer of success and longevity of the business.' He believes that 'having a constitution and involving the women in the family is a good idea as it helps to curtail the probability of conflicts.' The bottom line is clear: when in doubt, the interest of the business comes first, ahead of the family's interest! Let's see in the next chapter aspects of Mariwala's distinct style of leadership that make him a shaper.

Chapter 7

Decoding the Shaper

L eaders of Gen-Liberalization companies like Housing
Development Finance Corporation (HDFC), Larsen &
Toubro, Biocon, Kotak Mahindra and Marico, which took off
on a sustained growth path since liberalization, stand out
in the crowd for their efforts in shaping their organizations
into institutions. Among them is Harsh, the founder, and now
non-executive chairman of Marico.

So, what makes Harsh a shaper? What has been his role
in the shaping of Marico as an institution? We applied the
SPJIMR MBA framework to determine Harsh's role as an
institution builder (see Research Methodology).

PEOPLE RELATIONS

Institutions like IIM Ahmedabad, Khaira District Milk
Producers' Cooperative (Amul) and Tata Consultancy Services
among others share a remarkable characteristic—they have
been shaped by leaders unshakeably committed to achieving
success through people relations. Whether it is Ravi Mathai,

first director of IIM Ahmedabad; Verghese Kurien, builder of the Amul Cooperative; or the Kohli-Ramadorai duo, all of them invested in developing their people and in building beneficial networks for the good of their institution. It is this factor that underlies the axiom 'Men may come and men may go but the institution lives on after the builder.' With Harsh, it was his relations with his extended family that laid the foundation of his people skills.

Family: Harsh has always been close to his large joint family with a multitude of uncles and cousins living and working together. Living in this milieu helped him develop tact, patience and resilience. His deep commitment to quality stems from his father, in whose tenure Parachute coconut oil and Saffola edible oil were launched. Two generations of Mariwalas stayed in the same sprawling bungalow sharing a common kitchen, living room and dining area. Growing up in an expanding business family heightened Mariwala's sensitivity and ability to handle interpersonal relations. His entry into the family business as an intern helped provide the exposure to the nitty-gritty of handling business, better than what he could have learned in a business school. Harsh's appreciation for product quality stemmed from his experience at BOIL where he observed the family going the extra mile to ensure that both Parachute and Saffola were 'top quality' products. The innate sense for offering customers a quality product from the House of Mariwalas germinated during this period.

With commitment and enthusiasm, Harsh learned and came up with innovations for the business for which he was able to obtain consent from family elders, through artful persuasion rather than by using brinkmanship tactics. The family in turn, responded favourably, so long as they could influence the pace and investment value of the decisions. Early on in his internship, Harsh understood that 'patience pays' with the family. It took him a decade to fully implement his revolutionary idea of converting tin packs to plastic containers. Eventually, the differences in business outlook between him and the family grew as Harsh was eager to implement his vision for branding BOIL's consumer products, whereas his family seemed content in selling them as commodities. The separation of businesses was inevitable but Harsh was able to engineer the same without breaking away from either BOIL or his family. Neither was there any public acrimony nor resentment post the separation. His youngest uncle Kishore joined him as the co-founder of Marico.

Professional: Mariwala's ability to relate with people helped him develop the company's distributors, retailers, sales force and supply chain vendors into a formidable marketing asset. This relationship stood him in good stead during the company's hour of crisis when its survival was at stake. The dealer network responded warmly to his *'Parachute ki kasam'* call for support. Early in his business career, he leveraged this ability to derive first-hand customer insights on coconut and edible oils. Harsh could induct and lead a core team of talented executives from reputed companies, as an unknown MD of an inconspicuous family-managed concern, to collectively work on laying the foundation of the Marico of today. Infected with his deep conviction on the destination and path for the start-up, the team worked with him in the making of Marico as a reputed Indian emerging market FMCG corporation. It was this team, in tandem with the next level of senior managers, who drafted the Mission and Values document for presentation and finalization with the Board. Apart from himself, his uncle and subsequently his son, Rishab, Harsh got on board independent Board members with a reputation for upholding corporate governance who were accomplished corporate honchos with complementary business skills and networks. This is testimony to his ability to win over eminent professionals to guide the company on its tryst with destiny.

Conscious of his modest education—in the early days—that seemed disproportionately inadequate to achieve his ambitious goal of creating a leading Indian, branded FMCG company, Harsh sought out global and national consultants from whom he picked up the basics and nuances of business strategy and branding. Harsh had no pretensions about his need for learning and possessed the self-belief to have the best possible talent to work with him. He struck effective relationships with Prof. Bhandari and Prof. Charan when Marico had just come of age as a promising Indian consumer product venture. Harsh's relationship with Prof. Charan has withstood the test of time. So has his relationship with other key consultants who contributed to shaping his perspective on men and matters.

SHORT- VS LONG-TERM BEHAVIOUR

Business growth is like oxygen to Harsh, as he believes that without growth, stakeholders cease to create wealth. For

Mariwala, unlike some VC-driven new economy adventurers, growth means profits, not merely increase in volumes. A time gap between revenues and profits is, however, acceptable as long as the growth line is steeper than the loss line and there is visibility of profit.

Harsh instituted the model of a five-year strategic Business Plan for Marico, to be reviewed annually for an update, based on emerging factors. Although this may be a common practice in well-established companies, Harsh, the scion of a traditional business family, initiated this model for his new venture in 1990. This planning process provided for the achievement of short-term growth as well as for pivoting the plan for long-term goals to avail of emerging trends.

Long-term planning is evident in Marico's Values Statement, among the initiatives taken by Harsh, during the christening period of Marico. The statement affirms 'Profit Optimization' and not 'Profit Maximization'. The differentiation in the choice of the word was deliberate to signal that there would be no trade-off between quality and costs for maximizing short-term profits. Constant refinement in product features for customer benefits, in manufacturing processes and in MISs were clear commitments to the long term. Harsh understood that with continuous business growth, there was a need for professionals with values. As he is quoted saying, 'You can't take shortcuts. Quality, safety, product development matter and you have to ensure these things happen.'[26] These were commitments that had to be

---

[26]Pankaj Mishra, Outliers podcast, June 2018, Episode 13: Harsh Mariwala of Marico on his biggest failures and what he learned from them. Available at: https://podcast.factordaily.com/outliers-58-harsh-mariwala-of-marico-on-

made to realize the vision of an Indian, emerging market MNC in the FMCG sector.

A striking example of foregoing short-term benefits for long-term interests is seen in the company's policy for maintaining company stocks with distributors. The common practice in the FMCG industry is to push stocks to distributors, come month end. But Marico follows a programmed replenishment model based on demand and availability wherein stocks are supplied only at shortfall in benchmarked inventory.

Mariwala was clear on the future for Marico as a trusted Indian company marketing branded FMCG. It was his tryst with branding that put Marico on the trajectory of high profitable growth. He understood that brand value gets diluted with short-term measures like increased consumer promotions to handle aggressive targets or with defending against a well-funded new entrant, actions that can adversely impact long-term growth. He, therefore, worked to strengthen Parachute and Saffola as brands and extended brand reach over the years. While consistently pursuing a growth strategy, Marico has avoided falling prey to short-term tactics.

CRITICAL THINKING

Mariwala has applied uncommon sense whenever faced with challenges. It was not 'more of the same' with him, being content to grow coconut and edible oils as a commodity business, generating incremental growth with moderate

his-biggest-failures-and-what-he-learned-from-them/

profits, as had been the accepted family practice. Without forsaking the core values of the family business, Harsh brought in a fresh mindset. His 'uncommon sense' is seen in his actions towards making brands out of Saffola and Parachute. His intense sessions on branding with Professor Bhandari convinced him that branding was the way forward for Parachute and Saffola. What was simply an item for dining table discussion for the family like the brand success of Shalimar Oil in eastern India or of family friends Atul Choksey and Jignesh Dani, co-founders of Asian Paints, successfully outclassing competition through branding, became a matter of conviction for Harsh. He was very much in the milieu, yet thinking beyond it.

The branding odyssey was no cakewalk for Harsh. Its consequences meant taking crucial decisions like moving away from the parent company, recruiting senior achievers from professionally managed consumer product companies, creating a culture suitable for consumer brands and consulting with a panel of experts—actions inevitably leading to delinking ownership from management. All these decisions had a critical impact on the company. For instance, the five-year Business Direction plan for Marico clearly specified the FMCG product categories of wellness and health foods as domains for Marico to operate in, which also drew the line at product categories that Marico would not venture into, like shampoo and offerings taken up by MNCs. The basis for these decisions was the identification of Right to Win products, in which Marico could become a market leader by being the first- or second-choice brand through differentiation. As Harsh said, 'We were clear that we should be able to either offer something unique in terms of product formulation, pioneer some product or have a strong brand presence.' This was the strategic thinking used to define the battleground in terms of competitive advantage for Marico.

Another critical decision for Marico in recent years has been to set the organizational balance between traditional Engine 1 products marketed through conventional distribution channels and emerging Engine 2 products marketed over the digital platform. Engine 1 products comprise the core Parachute and Saffola brands that repiesent Marico's trademark foray into the world of branded FMCG. Despite reservation by some investors, Harsh was clear that there would be no slowdown in Marico's efforts for its Engine 1 products and it would continue to be attentive to mother brands Parachute coconut oil, the cash cow since inception, and Saffola edible oil. His insight was that the unbranded market for coconut oil was not insignificant in size and the switchover rate would be attractive for years to come.

Marico's R&D had a track record of coming up with value adding, Right to Win Engine 2 brand extensions for Parachute and Saffola, which gelled with current trends in consumer behaviour. Harsh banked on Saugata to steer Marico's R&D for Engine 2 products in addition to overseeing the growth of its Engine 1 range.

In another example of his critical thinking, Harsh treaded off the beaten path and practised the principle of merit without exception for all roles, including his own when Saugata was chosen to succeed Mariwala as MD and CEO. This was unusual because family businesses traditionally recruit qualified personnel for senior-level responsibilities, while equipping their own next generation with academic 'ammunition' from B-Schools as cover to take over from the parent. It is commonly understood and accepted that the top job would be occupied by the family.

Adherence to merit across the organization is rare among founders as the exhibition of loyalty is a comfort factor just as the attachment to family is a tempting weakness. Genuinely making way for an unrelated professional as successor is the ultimate example of placing company interest above family interest by the founder.

ORBIT-CHANGING BEHAVIOUR

It was Charandas, Harsh's father, who transformed the family business from trading to manufacturing. That was a significant orbit change. Under him, BOIL developed Parachute and Saffola as high-quality consumer oils. Converting these two oils to brands was the next change in orbit for Marico, which required knowledge and skill sets different from conducting a commodity-based manufacturing business.

Leading this change was Harsh, who learned marketing and branding from consultants, by reading and by observation and by working in the field, interacting with distributors, retailers and sales staff of BOIL, the channel and with customers.

Having understood the market and perceived gaps to fill in by innovation, Harsh initiated an integrated marketing effort starting with shifting focus from factory to consumer. He followed up on this learning by raising Marico's talent quotient, tightening manufacturing for cost with quality, transforming packing from dull tin containers to attractive plastic bottles and containers and reaching out to retail. Capping it all was a value proposition leveraging the RighttoWin differentiators of Parachute and Saffola. Harsh was successful in this marathon effort that left no stone unturned for achieving higher growth and increased profitability. Marico was recognized as a leading Indian branded FMCG company.

Gaining recognition as an Emerging Market MNC was the next orbit for Marico. Moving from one orbit to the next meant increasing the scope and scale of operations. At Marico, this led to more people, more products and greater diversity in operations, which would requiremore learning and adapting, in quick time, to handle emerging situations. Under Harsh's tutelage, the HR function enabled rather than disabled Marico to scale up at speed, with a mindset that actively supported the drive for expansion.

BREAKING DOWN BARRIERS

It requires passion and persistence to overcome barriers to growth, especially mindset barriers. Harsh faced such barriers in the course of his odyssey to 'brand' Marico. For example, his uncles' unwillingness to spend money on intangibles like brand building, requiring him to patiently explain and persuade them to come around to accept that branding Parachute and Saffola was the way forward for the company.

A key element of the branding exercise was the massive exercise of upgrading containers from old-fashioned tin to contemporary high-density polyethylene and then working with his R&D team on an innovative leak-proof cap. Harsh used his goodwill with distributors and dealers to patiently convince them into making the shift from tin to plastic. He lent credibility to his efforts by demonstration. Customer response to the upgraded containers vindicated his belief and successfully overcame their barriers. It further built up his image with the trade. Increased revenues and profits bore testimony to the benefits from this change.

Another instance of Harsh's ability to break down barriers was in recruitment of talent based on merit and backed by values. Attracting the best talent to Marico was initially difficult as BOIL had an image problem, being perceived as a traditional family business. However, Harsh overcame this obstacle with imagination by getting an advertising agency known for creativity to release a striking, placement ad vividly portraying Marico as a happening place for FMCG marketers to show their mettle. The promise implicit in the ad was reinforced during the interview by his credibility as the head of such an exciting company. Marico was heralded as a promising, new presence in the branded FMCG space. By recruiting and retaining high-quality talent to work with him from the start-up stage, Harsh yanked Marico from within the constraints of a family business to the new orbit of exciting professionalism.

LEVERS OF CHANGE

Harsh used the levers of change to make Marico a formidable emerging market consumer goods player. He leveraged the soft power of the HR function to change the face of Marico as a multitalented family of professionals bound by a common purpose, which fostered job empowerment and hierarchy-free, cross-functional interaction among employees. The Marico culture and values also meant doing away with attendance-related regulations for staff. Similarly, staff was authorized to self-determine their job-related expenses. The adherence to integrity was implicit. Everyone understood and appreciated that performance is linked to merit. Team working was actively encouraged. A lapse in value or slack in learnability could be cause for self-introspection and parting of ways. This was a significant path-breaking change in shaping the HR policy at the fledgling stage of a company, which was a conventional family business and not a VC-funded start-up.

Marico was among the earliest FMCG companies to deploy innovations in IT as a lever for accelerated growth. it customized software applications to monitor sales and inventory up to the retail level in real time, getting the distributor to invest in hardware. Being the largest buyer of coconuts, it got copra intermediaries on its online platform to provide quotes, update logistics and make payments. This initiative brought in cost savings of 2 per cent.

Harsh proactively played the lead role to create a collaborative, empowered organization and lead a TMT that collectively discussed and decided on strategic issues in consultation with the Board and individually took responsibility for outcomes. He also demonstrated his faith in merit by making way for a professional Mariconian to replace him as MD, thereby setting a powerful example for managing merit-based succession in a family-managed business. Employee empowerment was an article of faith at Marico, which served to sustain morale and motivation at high levels.

CYCLICAL LEARNING

The enterprise lifecycle of a venture from start-up to profitable sustainability requires differing competencies at different stages from the founder, who needs to learn how to align behaviour to meet the challenges at each stage. For instance, the shaper needs to change behaviour from 'doing everything' to 'getting things done' to 'leading the organization' to eventually 'influencing without authority.' Inability to transition from one stage to the next is the prime cause of enterprise stagnation, decay and exit.

Harsh learnt the knowledge, skills and attitude required to handle each stage of growth and shape Marico as an emerging market MNC. As Mariwala puts it, 'I understood that the ability to change gears from time to time is crucial for a successful business. Being nimble and agile, adaptable to a changing business environment is a necessity, which for many entrepreneurs is a difficult task. It is important for entrepreneurs to understand that while the process of starting a new business is significant, it is different from expanding it. Resources are of prime importance to a growing business.' Durable relations with mentors of the calibre of Prof. Charan helped negotiate the transitions.

Certain behavioural traits are necessary for founders to learn to transform from a leader to a shaper who influences without the crutches of authority, and are critical for a company to evolve as a business institution. Post his decision to hand over the day-to-day running of Marico to Saugata—evoking a clear 'Why' response—Harsh adopted a 'hands off, mind on' stance that reinforced his decision.

STAKEHOLDER ORIENTATION

The typical company tends to prioritize shareholder interest over that of other stakeholders as this approach is seen to maximize investor and founder valuations. Stakeholders of a listed company like Marico include founders, investors, Board members, employees, supply chain and distribution partners, coconut farmers and society. How does Marico serve the interests of all its stakeholders?

Investors: Profitable growth and high distribution of dividends has kept Marico's investors happy. Marico has consistently fared well in fulfilling this need for returns.

Board members: Marico has members on its Board with domain competence, governance exposure, and experience in managing family businesses and multinationals. Besides the family, Board members are independent directors who have served to increase the Board's effectiveness. Marico's Board has competently navigated through the issues and challenges faced by the company during the course of its evolution. Some of these include implementation of the code of conduct, creation of a separate company for the Kaya brand, succession planning at senior levels, mentoring senior teams, and acquisitions and divestments, besides a critique or feedback system to add value to business and brand strategy.[27]

Talent: The cornerstone of Marico's work culture is merit and empowerment. Empowerment is based on trust and

[27]Samar Srivastava, 'Forbes enriched the value chain of the company India,' 12 Jun 2014. Available at: https://www.forbesindia.com/article/boardroom/marico-3.0-from-singlebrand-to-diversified-consumer-goods/37958/1

belief in learning from failures. Such an environment breeds innovation and results in accountability. Add to this a top management mindset that rewards continuous growth from an organization with just five levels. In tandem, a sure recipe for attracting and retaining quality talent with a bias for generating excellent outcomes.

Distributors and Suppliers: By treating suppliers and distributors as genuine partners, Marico has enriched the value chain of the company. The MIS linkage has been designed to enable distributors to monitor data related to all their principals and not just Marico. The distributors readily consented to be integrated with the company's MIS system as Marico does not conform to the time-honoured practice of month-end dumping of stocks. The MIS also enables payment to vendors and distributors as per agreed norms. The company conducts programmes for farmers to improve the yield in their farms and ensures they are paid a fair price on time for the coconuts.

Society: Contributing to the good of society, neither the company nor its stakeholders pollute the environment. Marico's coconut collection centres provide cultivation-related information to the farmers. Outreach programmes focusing on scientific farming practices help raise farmer incomes. Additionally, Marico's Corporate Social Responsibility (CSR) contribution is based on mentoring and facilitating entrepreneurs to scale their venture for the benefit of society through the Marico Innovation Foundation. Giving back to society is important to Harsh.

In an interview with YourStory,[28] Harsh explained how he embarked on this journey: 'I wanted to give back to society, not just money or hospital or a school or college. I wanted to play a catalytic role apart from financial resources. This meant I needed to select something that was my passion, through which I could impact others and give my time to add value. I had four options actually—entrepreneurship, health, education and innovation.'

Marico Innovation Foundation: Harsh began with innovation, setting up the Marico Innovation Foundation (MIF), a non-profit organization funded from Marico's CSR kitty. The purpose of MIF is to 'work towards the cause of innovation by helping entrepreneurs effectively and efficiently scale their businesses and social organizations, thereby enhancing their economic and social value.' What qualifies as innovation—as against jugaad, which is born out of constraints—is scalability.

Priya Kapadia, Head of MIF, says it was at the Foundation that she 'realized that a symbiosis between business principles and social innovation can be the surest way of creating lasting impact for the betterment of society, as it enables us to bring in greater accountability and a stronger focus on benchmarking to all our causes. All our core programmes have been customized to enhance the aspects of innovation that we see as buildable.'

MIF's governing council has members like Dr R.A.

---

[28]Shradha Sharma, 'Ascent of an innovator: Mariwala's transformation from astute entrepreneur to business catalyst', yourstory.com. Available at: https://yourstory.com/2018/02/ascent-innovator-harsh-mariwalas-legacy-builds/

Mashelkar, former director general of the Council of Scientific and Industrial Research (CSIR); Rajeev Bakshi, strategist and marketing consultant; Ravi Venkatesan, engineer and social entrepreneur; and Anu Aga, business person and social worker. MIF works closely with over 25 organizations in 13 sectors to help overcome their scale-up challenges.

ASCENT Foundation: As part of his personal social responsibility, Harsh set up the ASCENT Foundation (Accelerating the Scaling up of Enterprises), a peer learning platform for growth stage entrepreneurs to meet and share their experiences.

Harsh observes, 'I started my business at a small pace and I realized that as you progress from small to medium to large size, entrepreneurs need to go on shifting their focus, role and processes; many entrepreneurs are not able to do so. Although good businesses, they are not able to grow beyond a certain scale. So, if I can play a role in helping others, then I'm using my experience in adding value to these entrepreneurs, who will get to scale further to benefit all stakeholders. When we can create an ecosystem of entrepreneurs we can learn from each other and from others who can then help. In that process they are able to grow. This is the value add by ASCENT. Nobody else was doing this.' ASCENT conducts educational events like how to raise funds from different routes, huddles, mixers and conclaves. Currently, ASCENT has about 350 entrepreneurs aggregating a turnover between ₹16,000 crore and ₹17,000 crore. The objective is to help entrepreneurs to scale up and add value to all stakeholders, including themselves, their employees, government and society.

Mariwala passionately led Marico's growth and success, demonstrating entrepreneurial strengths unique to a shaper. The Shapers MBA framework created by the authors of these series, emerged from an intense study of six different business organizations recognized as institutions in India to discern patterns as there may be. Not all parameters may be applicable to all the organizations with equal significance. Marico, recognized as a business institution in the FMCG sector, went on to chart its own unique and distinctive growth journey that came to be defined as the Marico Way, as we shall see in the next chapter.

Chapter 8

The Marico Way

Mariwala shaped Marico as a business institution in the course of three decades since the inception of the company as an independent unit. Earlier, the company existed as a subsidiary of the Mariwala family business, BOIL. With a life of its own, Harsh and his core team transformed the subsidiary from a competence-driven, shareholder value-generating company to a purpose-driven, stakeholder value-generating institution. What are some learnings on leadership and management that students and practitioners of management can gain by charting the life journey of Marico? What is the Marico Way of building a business institution?

Marico is a Gen-Liberalization company recognized as an institution in the Indian consumer goods sector. Over 90 per cent of Marico brands have been ranked among the top two in the category. The company has been delivering consistently high on key financial parameters—compounded annual growth rates of 16 per cent in turnover and 24 per cent in profits since inception, outperforming the Bombay Stock Exchange (BSE)

FMCG index.[29] The company has been recognized with various awards for its management practices, corporate governance and contribution to society. For instance, it was ranked in the top five BSE 100 Indian Companies and recognized for Excellence in Corporate Governance at the 15th Institute of Company Secretaries of India (ICSI) National Awards.[30] It figures high on the list of firms for which recruitment agencies like to work.

Since 2014, when Saugata succeeded Mariwala as the MD and CEO, the founder serves as non-executive chairman of the Board constituted majorly of independent directors with distinguished track records in relevant domains. The Board members are provided in advance with information required for taking decisions on the agenda. The company's decisions and actions reveal a deep commitment to all its stakeholders promoting some distinctive practices that have illuminated the Marico Way.

PURPOSE: BE MORE EVERYDAY

Every business has its What (business direction), Where (operational domains), When (targets) and Who (people). But it is the 'Why' question that is the most crucial. A sound answer captures the business's purpose and provides a robust foundation for the business to flourish. Mariwala defines Marico's purpose as the 'guiding principle that directs the business's actions: it is the reason underlying its existence,

---

[29]Based on: Ambit Capital Research
[30]Refer to: https://www.marico.com/page/DigitalReport2018-2019/awards.html

not just in the market, but in society. Our philosophy at Marico to 'Be more, every day' was created with this intention to transform in a sustainable manner the lives of all those we touch—customers, employees and suppliers—by nurturing and empowering them to maximize their true potential. We realize that as our stakeholders become conscious of Marico's higher purpose, it reverberates across the whole business ecosystem and the width of the potential only multiplies manifold.'[31]

Harsh had observed that over time, employees tend to become less engaged with the company they work for. The motivation for achieving the next 'raise' and for exercising greater power loses some of its potency with the passage of time. There is a craving for fulfilment beyond striving for wealth and slogging for ambition. Studies have shown the co-relation between engaged employees and satisfaction from the human desire to fulfil a higher purpose. What is applicable for employees applies to business partners too. For purpose to be meaningful, fairness and ethics in everyday behaviour continues to be a given at Marico, just as its emphasis on merit. Marico's Purpose 'Be more, every day' was adopted to engage the fraternity to give more of themselves in their daily lives and thereby create benefits for all in the ecosystem.

Marico's impact on society is channelled by the company's CSR activity to promote and mentor entrepreneurs and innovators, the agency being the MIF. Mariwala's belief that enabling the growth of social enterprises is the way to

---

[31]Harsh Mariwala, 'The Heart of the Matter', *The Hindu Business Line*, 18 July 2013. Available at https://www.thehindubusinessline.com/opinion/the-heart-of-the-matter/article22995005.ece

go, rather than donations, is institutionalized through the foundation.

'WIN WIN' WITH STAKEHOLDERS

Sustainability requires companies to realize that 'the sum of the parts is greater than the whole' and accordingly shape their attitude towards stakeholders, which in turn is reciprocated by the stakeholders. The interests of all are interlinked as it is in an ecosystem. Pursuing a 'Robbing Peter to pay Paul' approach does not ensure sustainability over time. There are enough examples of one-time stock market darlings being relegated to pariahs to vindicate this truism.

From its inception, Marico has consciously aligned the interests of all stakeholders to the common purpose of growth through mutual benefit. Marico's media, research team, PR and creative agencies participate in leadership training programmes and networking events that the company organizes. Farmers participate in schemes conducted by agri-experts for generating higher yields that enable them to obtain higher rates resulting in the company deriving benefits from higher productivity. The sales and inventory software package developed for distributors is an open software that they can use for all of their principals including Marico.

For employees, Marico has enunciated an Employee Value Proposition that results in all-round growth of its employees, who the company regards as 'members' of the Marico family. Decision-making is decentralized along with empowerment and responsibility. For a company generating a billion dollar-plus in revenues, the organization has just five levels. Not surprisingly, Marico is perceived as an exciting, contemporary, Indian FMCG player with international presence.

CUSTOMER CENTRICITY

Successfully confronting an existential crisis followed by its memorable victory over Hindustan Unilever for supremacy in branded coconut oil, Marico could have become complacent. However, judging by its subsequent performance, there has been no dilution in customer-centricity that is constantly reinforced by innovations, product quality, customer awareness programmes, extending reach and, overall, by raising brand value rather than by discounting.

The Marketing and Sales teams combine with the Market Research and Consumer Insight teams to track customer needs, changes in consumer behaviour, product innovations and competitor activities. The Board and Top Management are aware that the next billion dollar in revenues will not be majorly from serving customers with the same Engine 1 products. This is reflected by the reduced dependence on the core brands. Contribution from Parachute and Saffola have dropped from 100 per cent at Marico's inception to 43 per cent in 2019. Evolving customer trends in haircare, skincare and healthy foods will require a new range of products (Engine 2) made available beyond conventional channels. The organization is geared to respond to this opportunity.

EMPOWERING CULTURE

Fulfilling the purpose everyday requires a nurturing and

empowering culture. Empowerment starts with trust-generating measures that maximize staff involvement, like providing for a balance between professional work and personal needs. At Marico, there are no official 'office hours'. There is no roster for keeping track of the 'casual leave' taken. The HR norms also ensure that employees have sufficient space to innovate without being blamed for failure. In this way, employees are empowered to succeed or learn from their efforts and take responsibility for the outcome. And for guidance, access is open to anyone across roles, with no objections from superiors.

Selection processes adopted by HR raise the probability of recruiting employees who leverage such an environment for mutual good, for the company and themselves. Trust is the bottom line for such practices whether with employees or associates. When trust is violated, there is one remedy—severance from the company. HR also works on continuous reinforcement of company culture with 'imbibe while you are involved' activities.

FAMILY OWNED, PROFESSIONALLY MANAGED

While BOIL was a business owned by the Mariwala family, Harsh contributed as a family member in growing the consumer product division. He initiated the separation of disparate businesses without synergy and charted the way forward for the consumer products division. He ensured a harmonious, sensitive separation of the family businesses unlike many businesses, family controlled or otherwise, that make an ungainly public show of their differences. For Marico that was the first step off the starting bloc towards business sustainability.

In family businesses, the family tends to be the company and the company is the family. A major stumbling block to institutionalizing a first-generation family business can be the overwhelming role of the founder. Many long-term founders harbour the fear 'after me, the deluge' without realizing their own contribution to such a situation!

Marico has a TMT of accomplished professionals who jointly evolve, execute, review and revise strategic decisions under the leadership of the MD and CEO. The TMT practises Marico's signature cultural characteristics of meritocracy, values, transparency, discussion and timely decision-making. Criticism and politicking are a no-no since the company's inception, although critiquing and dissent are allowed. The TMT is encouraged to have a holistic perspective on management.

Further, in sharp contrast with Indian family businesses, Mariwala's choice of successor was the COO, his next-in-command, a professional unrelated to the family, who was chosen on merit for his abilities to maintain the growth of the mother brands and lead Marico's profitable growth in the emerging FMCG categories. In this context, it is relevant to draw attention to Securities and Exchange Board of India's ruling to separate the functions of chairman and Managing Director and to have one of them as a non-family member by April 2022.

BOARD MATTERS

Marico has grown consistently, with impressive business financials. Nearly 90 per cent of its brands are market leaders.

The company is recognized by the industry for its pioneering innovations in products and operations, for creating trusted brands and for being an employer of choice.

The Board has had an influential role in these achievements. Collectively, the members bring in a range of skills and exposure that have enriched the formulation of business direction for the company. The Board was involved in the exercise for defining Marico's Purpose, Culture and Values. It is conscious of actively fulfilling its oversight function.

While Mariwala, his uncle and son Rishab have a presence on the Board as family members, the majority of Board members are independent directors, who have been chosen for their relevance in the domains and skills to oversee a growing indian emerging market MNC in FMCG.

WALK THE TALK

A growth mindset in contrast to an attitude of complacency manifests in 'constantly managing the small changes and innovating. You are much more likely to try something new if you are already successful at making changes,' Professor Rosabeth Moss Kanter, faculty at Harvard Business School commented.[32] At Marico, innovation covers product and process enhancements, vendor and distributor growth on a continuing basis. Early on, Harsh had gotten wise to the reality of attracting and retaining quality talent by keeping them engaged in innovative assignments. For Marico, a key

---

[32]*Marico Annual Report for Year 2004-05*, p.68

descriptor of 'quality' talent is the ability to keep learning. To 'do what you say' is another ingrained belief among Mariconians, starting from the founder. Mariwala and his team have been able to embed in the organization that 'everything Marico believes in, Mariconians live by'. The culture does not provide for discretionary 'exceptions'. Mariconians understand that failing to match behaviour with talk results in loss of credibility and trust. Other Mariconian values are commitment to innovation, dedication to growth, trust comes with accountability, merit is the yardstick without exception and there are no escape buttons on accepting responsibility. This value system has served Marico well to propel it forward on a consistent growth curve.

MARCHING FORWARD

How long will coconut oil continue to be the bedrock for Marico? Is it now time to shift emphasis on Engine 2 products to serve emerging opportunities? Digital technology is changing shopping behaviour. What the popularity of TV achieved in creating visibility for consumer products in the 1990s, digital media is replicating for the millennial consumer-focused start-ups, who have yet to match the supply chain efficiencies of the established players.

Already, selling to the millennial of today is hugely different to selling to millennials two decades ago. The marketing and fulfilling approach for online consumer products is far removed from that for offline FMCG.

Observing the changing marketplace trends, one is tempted to proclaim: 'The old order changeth, yielding place to new. And God fulfils himself in many ways, lest one good custom should corrupt the world'. The five years since Saugata took the baton from Mariwala have not been more of the same in play—Marico has responded to the winds of change. Saugata is leading Marico's efforts in catching the attention and retention of the millennial market and churning a range of new products. This new growth avenue of Engine 2 products is expected to be in the vanguard for propelling Marico to touch the next billion dollars in revenues.

Saugata is aware of the challenge posed by funded FMCG start-ups energetically scaling, by plugging 5000-plus items on e-commerce portals, quickly withdrawing 'no demand' products and outsourcing distribution. That is why, he says, 'Although Marico is the incumbent, it must now display the "insurgent" behaviour of the 1970s to match the "tactechs" of the digital FMCG start-ups.' He believes, 'You can operate with a model which is digital advertising and visual advertising and get critical mass,' thereby creating the opening for Engine 2 products that range from premium hair nourishment to skincare, protein shakes and soups. Eventually, Marico foresees the more successful of these new products entering offline distribution channels for volume sales. Gupta has created a business unit in start-up mode for Operation Engine 2 products.[33]

The top management at Marico appears convinced that continuation of Engine 1 and concentration on Engine 2 products will get Marico to the $2 billion-plus milestone

[33]Suman Layak 'Remaking Marico: How Marico MD Saugata Gupta wants to disrupt the FMCG market with a host of new categories', ET Online, 13 October 2019

in the near future. Besides targeting the millennials, these products would further reduce dependence on coconut oil and safflower oil commodity cycles.

So is Marico at the crossroads? Says management and market research consultant, Rama Bijapurkar, 'Marico has built a successful business with solid brand platforms. Now, the question is that these platforms have a lot of spring and where will you spring and change your pace or growth trajectory?' Having set Wellness and Healthy Foods as the two broad platforms for portfolio development, Marico should be on track to ride successive consumer waves.

Epilogue

The initial meetings of the SPJIMR faculty team of co-authors and the lead author had set our minds working on the 'why', 'how' and 'what' of writing theis series of books. As we delved deeper, and explored institutions past and present, we drew on the example of Amul cooperative as an institution, Verghese Kurien as the institutional shaper and the years of its worthwhile existence, which helped us visualize the theme of this book series. It also explained the 'why' underlying this exercise. Apart from adding to the repertoire of knowledge on business management, the ideas are something that readers can 'buy into'. Some new economy entrepreneurs may hopefully get more inclined to re-look at their purpose and leadership style.

Deliberations on what should be the duration of such institutions concluded with setting the eligibility bar for Indian companies not later than the post-liberalization period that commenced in the early 1990s. This became the time-bound guideline for the 'how' factor. A starting requirement was the 'live-liness' of the shaper.

As for 'what' the project would involve, it was agreed that a combination of primary research and referenced secondary search, punctuated with regular discussions between the author duos, was the way to go. Having decided the framework for the book, a representative list of candidates was compiled.

For a book on Marico and Mariwala, the authors pondered on what should be the essence, the core on which to direct the spotlight, that best brings out the common theme of the book series? They decided that it would be the metamorphosis of Marico from a plodding caterpillar to a radiant butterfly—translated as its transformation from the mundane consumer products division of the parent firm, BOIL, to Marico, the vibrant flag bearer of consumer branding. Mariwala harnessed the power of marketing to achieve this transformation in the context of the FMCG sector in which the company operated. The strategic weapon from the marketing armoury he deployed was branding. He made mega brands of Parachute and Saffola, which were earlier being treated as mere commodities.

A caveat is due here: Butterflies are associated with glorious transformations during their life span. Most have short lives. Institutions as we know are long lasting. The parallel has only been drawn to highlight the dramatic change between the outlook of the earlier consumer products division handling Parachute and Saffola as commodities— equivalent to the caterpillar—and that of Marico, handling the same products as distinct brands that acquired leadership position—equivalent to the butterfly.

How has this institution maintained its exemplary performance? Harsh acknowledges his father Charandas' contribution in ensuring that both Parachute and Saffola as products are genuinely superior to competition in terms of purity, clarity and aroma. Branding to Harsh was the means to enhance customer benefits while retaining product superiority. It is a truism that FMCG demands constant attention to brand reinforcement to ward off competition and changing customer trends and Harsh clearly understood this.

He followed a focused brand strategy of keeping away from the terrain of MNCs; hair oils and edible oils used in Indian cuisine are not represented in the product basket of global companies. Marico's competitors were more regional than national, whereby brand-related expenses were manageable. The only occasion on which this equilibrium was upset was when Lever chose to acquire Parachute. Marico's successful fight back is the stuff that makes business history. It brought to light Mariwala's 'ne'er say die' spirit, and his tremendous ability to marshal company and partner manpower resources to wage a 'do or die' war with the mighty aggressor.

The sustainability of the market leaders, Saffola and Parachute, reflects the calibre of Marico's marketing function. Affirms Rahul Bajaj, Managing Director, Bajaj Auto, 'I regard Mariwala as one of the biggest marketing brains.'[34] It is also a tribute to Marico's enabling culture.

Saugata, his successor as MD and CEO, has been able to adapt to the changed environment in which FMCG companies operate today. It is true that over time, consumer behaviour has noticeably changed in personal grooming and food habits. It will continue to do so. Rising discretionary income in tandem with more options is one aspect of this

[34] *The Hindu Business Line*, 'Mariwala mantra ignites Baja Auto', 27 November 2018. Available at: Mariwala mantra ignites Baja Auto, thehindubusinessline. com, 27 Nov. 2018

change. The other significant cause is the influence of the millennials living in a more connected world. Strategic brand expert Shombit Sengupta sums up the impact of the digital age on consumer goods, 'In the digital era, consumer attitude and behaviour have become extremely intuitive.' Saugata interprets this to mean that the innovation cycle worldwide, especially for FMCG has shrunk to barely 60 days as against several months earlier. Trends originating abroad travel to India more quickly. 'So, we have to be more entrepreneurial and agile with a higher innovation velocity,' he adds.

Marico, acknowledged as a sustainable and profitable player driving innovation in the traditional offline FMCG sector, has been quick to respond to the online FMCG consumer with Engine 2 products marketed through e-commerce and upmarket retail outlets. It has introduced new verticals that cover male grooming, premiumization of hair nourishment, health foods, and skincare that includes value-adding extensions and a new range of Kaya products.

Currently, mother brands Parachute and Saffola, which initially accounted for 100 per cent of Marico sales, today constitute less than 44 per cent of Marico's turnover. Although, the brands continue to grow with deeper reach into the hinterland and more users finding it affordable, it is due to faster growth in the new verticals that Marico's dependence on the founding brands has been reducing in recent years. As Saugata informs, 'Marico is aiming to bring down the share of mother brands to 30 per cent even as company revenues grow.'

Mariwala is also on the same page as Saugata. He is aware that the skill set for institutionalizing high growth in

Engine 2 products is not the same as that for the backbone Engine 1 brands. This is a different 'ball game.' Under Saugata's stewardship, Marico is taking strides in staking its presence in the new generation Engine 2 products. Twelve acquisitions in 12 years have accelerated the shift. Saugata is nurturing this activity in new venture creation mode.

The non-executive chairman keeps himself updated with regular reports, besides meeting the TMT once a month. He also chairs Board meetings, and in that role, oversees the continuity of Marico's business direction. His successor shares his perspective of not taking gen-next Marico along the garden path of vaulting revenues with declining profits or at the cost of deeper dilution of equity, which is characteristic of new-genre ventures in general.

Mariwala drove the transition of Marico from a commodity-oriented SME to an emerging market corporation, equipped with an inexhaustible yen to learn, an empowered TMT and his network of consultants. Saugata, equipped with Marico's purpose and values, and backed by his own competence and that of the TMT, is determined to reap the opportunities derived from Engine 2 products, while exploiting the cash flow benefits of Parachute and Saffola.

Meanwhile, Mariwala continues to add value by his 'hands off, mind on' presence. The role captures his ability to reinvent himself, from entrepreneur and founder to business head and now, a guide and mentor.

Marico's journey continues...fulfilling its purpose to society, being 'more everyday' to all.

Appendix

Research Methodology: Shaper's MBA Grid

A section on research approach and methodology seems out of place in a practice-oriented book, which aims to guide the modern-day manager and leader to be the shaper of an organization that can outlive most of its peers, and be hailed as an institution for its actions. While the book aims to be practitioner relevant—given the ambitious goal of studying six different organizations recognized as institutions in India to discern patterns—the research project was guided by a theoretical construct that was the result of serious deliberation and iteration. We termed this construct 'Shaper Mindset-Behaviour-Action (MBA) Grid', which is an important contribution, as it has the potential to act as a beacon for other researchers interested in and working in the field of leadership and organizational behaviour in the Indian context.

As such, we decided to 'relegate' the research approach and methodology to an appendix section, rather than use a book chapter for the same. The advantage of an appendix is that it can be skipped by those disinterested in the research approach itself without much loss of continuity in narrative. At the same time, it seemed apt to present serious researchers—who seek to further the research agenda on the theory and practice of institution-building—with a thorough understanding of the mindset and action patterns of institution builders under the directions of the chairman and Board.

Again, unlike the conventional research methodology section in an academic paper, we shall seek to keep this section light, highlighting the 'What', 'Why' and 'How' of our research in language, which will appeal to the lay reader, as much as to the seasoned academic.

THE 'WHAT'

The Shapers Research project owes its genesis to a serendipitous discussion amongst a few SPJIMR faculty members in 2018 on the distinction between organizations and institutions, and the distinction between their leaders. Discussion veered around Indian companies that feature in the Fortune Global 2000 list. There were about 50, including those like Reliance Industries (in the top 200 list) and TCS (in the top 500 list). There was consensus—tentative at this stage— that not all these organizations were 'institutions'. Also, while these organizations are aspirational to several MBA students who seek to find jobs with them, they offer little hope to the sceptic who is convinced about the mortality of corporations.

An influential piece of research in 2012 by Professor Richard Foster from Yale University, for instance, posited that the average lifespan of a company listed in the S&P 500 index of leading US companies has decreased by more than 50 years in the last century, from 67 years in the 1920s to just 15 years today.[35] Another study found the timespan of business survival to be merely 10 years.[36]

Given that most Indian businesses have emerged post the opening up of the Indian economy in 1991 and yet face multiple business challenges in the current uncertain and volatile business environment, the question that emerged was: 'Which of these organizations will survive long enough? Which Indian businesses are institutions?'

At this stage, we defined the term 'institution' as an organization that had at its core certain universally accepted values and norms for which it was revered; an organization that had withstood the test of time—having been established within a decade or two since Independence—and seemed to possess an innate resilience to be able to withstand multiple business challenges, having already survived several such challenges in the last several decades.

As we began to identify some of the organizations that qualified as institutions, as well as the factors that distinguished them from others, there was a Eureka moment in the realization that the phenomenon of institution-building is deeply linked to the leadership experience that each one goes through. In particular, we realized that the hypotheses for the research project, were it a conventional one, could very well read as follows:

---

[35]Refer to https://www.bbc.com/news/business-16611040
[36]Refer to https://fortune.com/2015/04/02/this-is-how-long-your-business-will-last-according-to-science/

H1: The number of years an organization survives is linked positively to leadership performance.

H2: The ability of an organization to withstand business volatility and severe business challenges is linked positively to leadership performance.

H3: The reputation that an organization carries is linked positively to leadership performance.

Needless to say, our preliminary research into institutions was guided by a literature review of scholarly work on institution-building, ranging from Powell, Arie de Geus, Di Maggio, Meyers and Rowan, to Indian scholars like Udai Pareek.

This then led to the question: What sort of leadership performance will qualify for such transformation of ordinary organizations into venerated institutions? The obvious answer was 'Transformational' leadership of a sort that transcends the current notion of leadership, as enunciated by Goleman, Moss Kanter and others—a leadership that not only transforms, but rather 'shapes' the organization into an institution. Such leaders may be called 'Shapers'. We also realized that just as there are only few organizations that may make it to a list of 'institutions,' there are few business leaders who may qualify as 'Shapers' of institutions.

This led us to an additional hypothesis:

H4: Leadership mindset, behaviours and actions undertaken by 'Shapers' are unique and distinct from those of the leaders.

We thought we were on to something interesting with this discovery. The next obvious question was: Could we—a group of interested researchers—work on a set of Indian organizations that *we* could identify as institutions, using a commonly accepted set of parameters? The set of such institutions need not be exhaustive. However, they need to conform to the parameters laid out, and should not be deemed questionable by the set of researchers working on the project, which now had a name—the SPJIMR Shapers Project. Can such institution building be studied in the context of the leaders, who, as Shapers, shaped and created them in a manner such that they have become enduring? Could we study and glean a set of uniform mindsets, behaviours and actions that would set these leaders apart from other leaders who are non-Shapers? And how do these Shapers shape their organizations into institutions? This then leads to the second aspect of our research: Why did we want to do this?

THE 'WHY'

Well, we could advance a large number of great-sounding explanations for why we undertook this research project, such as: 'We wanted to understand the mindsets and actions of Shapers so that it can help create shapers for the future' or, 'We want to make a difference to Indian management discipline and practice.'

These reasons are valid and good to conduct any such research. However, as every well-intentioned researcher in the field of social science will testify, we undertake research when the theme excites us. It helps us uncover phenomenon of which we have little understanding, but wish to unravel for ourselves. In the process, we do help set the research agenda for others as well.

In this case, it made sense as we could discern hints of a pattern emerging even as we began to do our preliminary research based on secondary data. We realized that rather than talking about leadership types in an anecdotal fashion, we could possibly decipher a method to such transformational leadership—not consciously agreed upon by those who practise it, but present all the same, waiting to be discovered and possibly even replicated.

In particular, what excited us were questions like:

▸ How does one distinguish an institution from an organization, even if the key metrics used to map organizational performance are similar, that is, involve deeper qualitative questions than merely looking at quantitative metrics? Thus, for instance, why should Reliance not feature in our list, even though it is one of the top Indian companies on the Fortune Global 2000 list.

▸ What transforms an organization into an institution? (The emphasis was on the process and not the outcomes.)

▸ What mindsets, behaviours and actions set a Shaper apart from a leader? This would entail a deep qualitative analysis, which could form the basis for a new theoretical construct, called the 'Shaper' construct.

▸ How and when does a leader qualify as a Shaper?

These questions also became the 'Why' or the 'Purpose' of our research. In the process, if we are able to expedite the transformation of some business organizations into institutions through their leaders adopting the right 'Shaper' mindset, that will be a happy, albeit unintentional, consequence of this book and project.

This leads us to our final question: How do we manage to undertake and bring this project to fruition?

THE 'HOW'

The process of shortlisting the tentative candidate organizations for the research project was undertaken by a small group, comprising of the authors—including the lead author—R. Gopalakrishnan—and Ranjan Banerjee, the dean of SPJIMR. A set of six institutions were initially shortlisted, with the understanding that a second round of other institutions could be worked on at a later stage. The institutions shortlisted in the first round included, in alphabetical order: Biocon, HDFC, Kotak, L&T, Marico and TCS. The methodology we sought to use in the project was a case study approach, involving in-depth interviews and triangulation. The project was then presented to the publisher, and approval was sought.

Each co-author, well-respected academics in their own right, began with carrying out background research on their subject of study—both the Shaper and the institution. In the case of at least one book in the series—TCS_we researched two shapers for the same institution.

We deliberated, discussed and arrived at the idea of a 'framework' that could be used to explore the main hypotheses. This was named the SPJIMR MBA Research Grid. The contents of the grid itself were arrived at through an iterative process of refinement as the research progressed.

In the initial stage, the grid was visualised as a 9×9 matrix with managers, leaders and shapers as distinct agents along task and process dimensions. The task dimensions considered were: Managing the Core; Preparing the Future and Creating the Future. Along the process dimension, managers were hypothesised as focusing on Policies and Processes, Leaders as focusing on Performance, while Shapers would focus on People. Juxtaposing the task and process dimensions, we arrived at a set of nine unique actions, which would set apart Shapers from Leaders and Managers.

In Stage 2, we refined this further to arrive at an 8×3 matrix. The vertical dimension (the columns) looked at Shapers' MBA, while the horizontal dimension (the rows) looked at the MBA categories broadly based on the 4Ps: Purpose, People, Policies and Processes. Shapers were identified in terms of their mindset along eight dimensions: People Relations, Short-term and Long-term focus, Critical Thinking, Orbit Shifting, Breaking Barriers, Levers of Change, Cyclical Learning and Stakeholder Orientation. We reproduce the MBA grid below.

The next step was to seek in-depth interviews with the 'Shapers' of these institutions, as also with multiple stakeholders, who could shed light on various dimensions of the shaper in question and their institution. While we decided and planned for the interviews, the idea was clear: these books were not meant to be hagiographies. While there were protagonists within the case study approach who were the Shapers, the 'heroes' were clearly the institutions, which had withstood the test of time, and made a distinct contribution to nation-building. Again, it was a conscious decision not to discuss the warts et al. of the Shapers, the reason being that we are interested in understanding the positive mindset that contributes to the building of a Shaper—an individual who, despite largely having an unblemished track record, is nevertheless as human as any of us in terms of frailties and vulnerabilities. Nowhere then, should the book be construed as an attempt to idolize a human being with a larger-than-life image.

Each researcher conducted at least three such interviews with different people associated with the shaper and/or the institution in question. Some of us met our protagonists more than once as well. The questions used to test the hypotheses included some generic questions, as also others, specific to the particular institution or Shaper. These included questions that revolved around institution-building, such as:

▸ How did you set the organizational vision, values, and performance expectations?
▸ How do you attract, retain and enhance talent within your organization?
▸ What is the purpose of leadership? How do you communicate with your workforce?
▸ How do you arrive at and institutionalize the core values of the organization?
▸ What is the role of 'out-of-the-box' thinking and an entrepreneurial mindset for any organization? How do you ensure that such a mindset gets internalized into the DNA of the institution?

- How do you and your senior leadership team guide and sustain the organization?
- How do you develop future leaders, measure organizational performance, and create an environment that encourages ethical behaviour and high performance?
- What are the institution's core competencies, work systems and designs that help create value for customers?
- How do you identify the organization's blind spots in achieving long-term organizational success and sustainability?
- What specific processes in institution building have you undertaken?
- How have you addressed succession planning in your organization?

There were other questions pertaining to each Shaper, which sought to explore key facets of their life that helped 'shape' the Shaper, starting from their childhood as well as their role models, etc. Another interesting question posed to the Shapers was: If they were given another three to five years at the helm, what would be the key 'unfinished' agenda that they would want to address?

All these questions helped glean the Shaper's mindset, behaviour and actions relating to specific aspects of institution building. We probed three specific areas: Building the institution, sometimes from scratch; seeing it through troubled times and changing the course. The idea was threefold: understanding the context, understanding the leader and understanding the institution.

The book chapters have also been aligned accordingly: The initial chapters set the context in which the organization developed, while the next set of chapters look at the life and key influences on the shaper, as also specific aspects of the Shaper's mindset, behaviour and actions. The last set of chapters cover the institution—what makes it qualify as one, the salient features of an institution and understanding the future of the institution.

FIGURE 1: SPJIMR SHAPER's
MINDSET-BEHAVIOUR-ACTION GRID

SPJIMR SHAPER MINDSET-BEHAVIOR-ACTION GRID		
Mindset	*Behaviour*	*Action*
People relations: Respectful to others	Sensitive and empathetic to others	Engages with people and nurtures them
Short vs long term: Both are equally important	Encourages to deal with the immediate, while silently considering the long term	Acts on the immediate decisively to get results creating the impression of small wins, so as to look forward to and work towards a big 'victory' in the future.

Critical thinking: Considers options and their pros/cons in mental evaluation	Encourages discussion and debate with an open-mindedness	Acts with precision and demands accountability
Orbit Changing: Constant evaluation of which orbit change will benefit the organization	Tosses around and debates the risks and rewards of orbit change, almost appearing indecisive	Demonstrates single-minded commitment once a decision is made
Break Barriers: I have the freedom to act if I am willing to steer through obstacles	Identifies the obstacles and seek the best way to deal: break it, go around it, navigate it	Once the path is clear, pursues with an Arjuna-like determination
Levers of change: Action is within my reach: must change complacency to the aspirational mindset	Debates and seeks ways out to unlock organization from negative hooks while attaching positive hooks	Presses for action and change in a disciplined manner
Cyclical learning: Action–Observation–Benchmark Review–Act again	Insists on a systems approach of cyclical learning	Ensures organization-wide deployment of an accepted system

Stakeholder Orientation: What is good for the stakeholder is good for the institution and hence, for us	Constantly understanding customer and community perspective	Always acts by keeping in mind multiple stakeholder interests

Acknowledgements

The faculty at SPJIMR bring with it exposure to industry. There is first-hand knowledge of how companies operate, warts and all. Deep interest in the evolution of enterprises from a start-up to a multinational corporation stage cuts across functional specialization. In this environment, undertaking a research-cum-practice project based on the theme of this book—to distil management insights on how shapers build institutions—received wholehearted support from the institute. Led by Dean Ranjan, who was deeply engaged in the key conceptual phase and maintained a lively interest thereafter.

As the faculty involved in this project, we must thank each other for the hours of discussions during 'work-in-progress' sessions, devoted to contributing knowledge and references, not excluding notes on enjoyable incidental experiences! From one author to the other, salute your timely interventions for overcoming the writer's plod!

This project would not have seen the light of day were it not for the publishers, Rupa. Appreciation is due to the Rupa team for the painstaking editorial work and imaginative cover design.

This book is about Marico and its shaper Harsh Mariwala. We are thankful to the people at Marico whom we met to gather information and knowledge on how Marico became an institution. Saugata, as Board member, MD and CEO of the family-owned and professionally managed company, provided his perspective on how Marico's consumer products continue to be relevant to the next generation. Marico's Chief Technology Officer Sudhakar Mhaiskar explained how Marico derived competitive advantage by enabling the supply chain and distributor channel with MIS. Rubina D'Silva's efficient assistance for the project deserves recognition. And, of course, special thanks to Harsh, the focus of this project!

We must also mention the debt of gratitude we owe to our families for their 'no quid pro quo' support through the inevitable 'ups and downs' experienced during the course of writing the book and to our colleagues with whom we discussed the 'subject' at various stages over multiple cups of tea, coffee and healthy snacks.